When Hope Springs New

Books by Janette Oke

Another Homecoming* / Tomorrow's Dream*
Celebrating the Inner Beauty of Woman
Dana's Valley†
Janette Oke's Reflections on the Christmas Story
The Matchmakers
Nana's Gift
The Red Geranium
Return to Harmony*

CANADIAN WEST

When Calls the Heart　*When Breaks the Dawn*
When Comes the Spring　*When Hope Springs New*
Beyond the Gathering Storm

LOVE COMES SOFTLY

Love Comes Softly　*Love's Unending Legacy*
Love's Enduring Promise　*Love's Unfolding Dream*
Love's Long Journey　*Love Takes Wing*
Love's Abiding Joy　*Love Finds a Home*

A PRAIRIE LEGACY

The Tender Years　*A Quiet Strength*
A Searching Heart　*Like Gold Refined*

SEASONS OF THE HEART

Once Upon a Summer　*Winter Is Not Forever*
The Winds of Autumn　*Spring's Gentle Promise*

SONG OF ACADIA

The Meeting Place*　*The Sacred Shore**
The Birthright*

WOMEN OF THE WEST

The Calling of Emily Evans　*A Bride for Donnigan*
Julia's Last Hope　*Heart of the Wilderness*
Roses for Mama　*Too Long a Stranger*
A Woman Named Damaris　*The Bluebird and the Sparrow*
They Called Her Mrs. Doc　*A Gown of Spanish Lace*
The Measure of a Heart　*Drums of Change*

———

Janette Oke: A Heart for the Prairie
Biography of Janette Oke by Laurel Oke Logan

*with T. Davis Bunn　　†with Laurel Oke Logan

01B

Janette Oke

CANADIAN ✤ WEST

When Hope Springs New

BETHANYHOUSE

MINNEAPOLIS, MINNESOTA

When Hope Springs New
Copyright © 1986
Janette Oke

Cover design by Jen Airhart

Published by Bethany House Publishers
A Ministry of Bethany Fellowship International
11400 Hampshire Avenue South
Bloomington, Minnesota 55438
www.bethanyhouse.com

Printed in the United States of America by
Bethany Press International
Bloomington, Minnesota 55438

ISBN 0-87123-657-5
ISBN 0-7642-2535-9 (mass market)

Dedicated with love and respect
to my youngest sister,
Sharon Violet Fehr,
another proof of the old saying,
"last but not least."
I appreciate her faith
and her dedication.
This comes with love—
to her, to her husband Richard,
and to Shawna, Eric and Amy.

JANETTE OKE was born in Champion, Alberta, during the depression years, to a Canadian prairie farmer and his wife. She is a graduate of Mountain View Bible College in Didsbury, Alberta, where she met her husband, Edward. They were married in May of 1957 and went on to pastor churches in Indiana as well as Calgary and Edmonton, Canada.

The Okes have three sons and one daughter and are enjoying the addition of grandchildren to the family. Edward and Janette have both been active in their local church, serving in various capacities as Sunday school teachers and board members. They make their home near Calgary, Alberta.

Contents

Chapter One

Uprooted

"Is it much farther?"

I felt like a small child asking again, but I really could not help myself. My whole being seemed to be in a state of agitation as we topped each hill, and the settlement was still not in view.

Wynn smiled understandingly. "Not too far," he comforted.

He had been saying that for quite a while now.

"How many hills?" I asked, hoping to pin him down to an answer that I could understand.

Now he didn't just smile, he chuckled. "You sound like a kid asking—'How many sleeps?'" he teased me.

Yes, I did sound like a kid. We had been on the trail for what already seemed forever. My common sense reminded me that it really hadn't been that long—four days, to be exact—but it felt like weeks.

Wynn reached out and squeezed my hand. "Why don't you ride for a while again?" he asked me. "You've walked enough now. You'll tire yourself out. I'll see what I can find out from the guide."

He signalled the driver of the lumbering team to stop and helped me up to a semicomfortable position on a makeshift seat. We resumed forward motion as he moved on down the line of wagons to seek out the guide of our small, slow-moving expedition.

He wasn't gone long, and then, without even slowing the wagon, he swung himself up beside me.

"You'll be happy to know that we should be there in about forty-five minutes," he said. Giving my shoulders a hug, he hopped down and was gone again.

Forty-five minutes! Well, I would manage somehow, but that still seemed like a long time.

During our four days of travel I had acquired aching bones, a sunburned nose, and a multitude of mosquito and blackfly bites. But it wasn't these irritations that had me troubled the most.

I realized that my agitation, that hollow, knotted spot in the center of my stomach, was all due to my fear of the unknown. I had not been nearly as frightened when I had come with Wynn to our first Northern outpost. Then I had been a new bride, eager to share the adventures of my Mountie husband.

I was still eager to share the adventures with Wynn, but this move was different. I had learned to know and love the Indian people at Beaver River. I had left behind not only the known but the loved. Now I had to start all over again.

I don't believe I was afraid that I would not be

able to make new friends. What worried me was how well I would be able to get along without my *old* friends. I was going to miss Nimmie so much. Surely there was not another person like her in all of the Northland. I would even miss Evening Star and Mrs. Sam and Little Dear and Anna. I would miss Wawasee and Jim Buck and my other students. I would miss the familiar Indian trappers, the simple homes I had visited so often, the curling wood-smoke, even the snarling dogs. Tears welled up in my eyes and slid down my cheek again. *I must stop this*, I chided myself, as I had done so many times already on the trail. *I will have myself sick before I even arrive.*

I pushed my thoughts back to safer ground, making myself wonder what our new home at Smoke Lake would be like. Well, I would not need to wonder for long. Wynn had said forty-five minutes, and the minutes were ticking by, even though slowly, with each rotation of the squeaky wheels.

Home again, I exulted inwardly, *after these days and nights on the trail!* I was looking forward to a nice hot bath and a chance to sleep in a real bed. Mosquito netting on the windows and a door to close for some privacy would seem like a luxury after this trip—with its heat, rain, and wind, by turn; with its steep hills, flat marshland, dusty trails, and soggy gumbo. Well, it would not be long now.

I looked at the sky. Perhaps we had had our last rain shower four hills back. The sky above me was

11

perfectly clear. *Surely it can't cloud over and drench us again in just forty-five minutes of time—probably thirty-five by now.* Even as I reasoned with myself, I wasn't completely convinced of our safety against another storm. Some of them had seemed to come upon us with incredible swiftness. I fervently hoped we would arrive at the new settlement in dry clothes. I hardly had anything left fit to wear. I was anxious to get out my washtubs and scrub up the wet and soiled things we had been stashing away in the wagon. They would be ruined if I didn't get at them soon.

The driver stopped to rest the team, and I climbed down from the wagon again. At least when I was walking, my anticipation was being channeled into something. I debated whether I should walk ahead of the team where I felt the risk of being run over at any minute, behind the team, where I would be forced to swallow trail dust, or off to the side where the walking was even more difficult. I decided to follow the team. I would lag far enough behind to let the dust settle a bit.

While I waited for the team to resume, I strolled to the side of the trail and looked around for signs of berries. I hoped there would be some in our area. Many of my canning jars were empty, and I did want to fill them again before another winter.

The area did not look promising.

There's lots of land around here, I assured my-self. *There could be many good berry patches.*

Kip came bounding up. In contrast to me, he thoroughly enjoyed the trip and all the new things there were to investigate. I had hardly seen him all day. He ran this way and that, ahead and behind, only coming back occasionally to check and make sure I was still traveling with the wagons.

I patted his head and was rewarded with generous waves of his curly tail. He licked my hand, then wheeled and was gone again before I even had time to speak to him.

Wynn dropped back, bringing with him a canteen of water.

"Need a drink?" he asked, and I suddenly realized I was thirsty. I smiled my thanks and lifted the canteen to my lips. The water was tepid, not like the refreshing water from our cabin well. Still, it was wet and it did help my thirst.

"We will soon be there," Wynn informed me. "I think it would be good to slip the leash on Kip. The village dogs might be running loose."

"He's gone again," I answered, alarmed. "He was here just a minute ago and then he ran off."

"Don't worry," Wynn assured me; "he won't be far away."

He was right. At the sound of Wynn's whistle, Kip came bounding through the underbrush at the side of the trail. His coat was dirty and tangled with briers and leaves, his tongue was lolling out the side of his mouth from his run, but he looked contented, perhaps even smug, about his new adventures.

I couldn't help but envy him. There was no concern showing in his eyes, like I must surely have been showing in mine.

Wynn slipped the leash on Kip and handed it to me. "I'm expected to be up at the front of the wagons when we enter the village," he stated simply. "Would you like to walk with me?"

I hesitated, not knowing what I wanted to do. I would like Wynn's support; still, I hated to walk into that new village like I was on display. I disliked the thought of all of those staring eyes.

"I think I'll just stay back here with Kip," I mumbled. "He won't fuss as much if he isn't in the center of the commotion."

Wynn nodded. I think he might have guessed my real reason.

The wagons up ahead had paused on the brow of the hill. I knew without even asking that just down that hill lay our new settlement—our new home. I wanted to see it, yet I held back in fear. How could one be so torn up inside, wanting to run to see what lay before, yet holding back from looking, all at the same time?

Without comment, Wynn reached forward and took my hand, then bowed his head and addressed our Father simply, "Our Father in heaven, we come to this new assignment not knowing what is ahead. Only You know the needs of these people. Help us to meet those needs. Help us to be caring, compassionate and kind. Help Elizabeth with all the new adjustments. Give her fellowship and friendships. Give her a ministry to the people, and keep us close to one another and to You. Amen."

I should have felt much better after Wynn's prayer, and I guess I did, but it was also another reminder of all the new things and experiences lying ahead.

I smiled at Wynn to assure him that I was fine. The wagons were moving again. We turned to follow, Wynn crossing the ground in long strides that would soon carry him out in front where he was expected to be.

I hesitated, holding in check the impatient Kip. The dust could settle some before I followed. There would be much commotion in the village at the coming of the new law enforcer. Everyone would be out to check him over. I was in no hurry to be thrust into the center of the staring throng.

Chapter Two

Smoke Lake

There it was—our new village stretching out before us on the floor of the forested valley. Wynn was right. It was larger than Beaver River. It was also more primitive and scattered in appearance. Wynn was right again. Yet it did not seem to be properly named. In the hazy stillness of the summer afternoon, not one of the many village homes had smoke ascending from the chimney.

I stood and let my eyes wander over the small, roughly constructed houses. Which one was ours, the one we would call home? In Beaver River our cabin had been set apart from the settlement. I let my eyes travel to the west, then the east, then the north and south. I could find no cabin located on the outskirts of the little village.

I found myself searching then for the sign of a garden. Surely someone in the village must wish to plant. But no, I could find nothing that looked like a cultivated area.

Even from this distance the small cabin homes looked shoddy and ill-kept. Compared to our homes in Beaver River, these looked like shacks. The large building in the center, which I assumed was the trading post, also looked hurriedly slapped together and run-down. Disappointment welled up within me.

For a moment I wished I could turn around and head back to the village I knew and loved. There I would be welcomed with softly curling woodsmoke. I would find a well-constructed, well-stocked trading post. I would discover my comfortable cabin at the outskirts of the village. I would be welcomed by neighbors and friends with gardens and berry patches.

Kip did not share my longings. He pulled forward on the leash and reminded me with a whine that I was to follow the wagons down the dusty, winding hill.

I broke from my reverie and started my descent. Already I could hear the village dogs as they set up their frenzied barking to announce the coming of strangers. Wynn's crated dog sled team, which rode the second wagon, responded to the howls. What a noise they all made!

Amid the din caused by the dogs, there were a few shouts and hellos, and arms were lifted in greeting. The first wagon was already rolling to a stop, boiling dust whirling in around it.

I pulled back on Kip's leash. I wanted some of the excitement to die down before I entered the village.

I saw a larger rock at the side of the trail in the shade of the tall pine trees. I led Kip to it and sat down to watch the milling around in the village below us. Kip whined and strained at the leash until I commanded him to be quiet and to lie down. He obeyed, rather reluctantly, and I turned my eyes back to the scene below.

It was several minutes before the wagons moved forward again. They stopped before a very small cabin with a sagging roofline, and I saw Wynn signal the men to begin unloading our crates and boxes.

Surely there must be some mistake! I thought. *That cabin isn't large enough to house Wynn's office, let alone our household too.*

Then a new thought passed through my mind. *No, we couldn't possibly be expected to live in that. It must be that our cabin is not ready, and we need to make do with temporary quarters.*

The unloading continued, and I saw Wynn look toward our hill. I knew he was searching for me, wondering what was taking me so long. I lifted my arm to let him know I was fine and coming to join him, and Kip and I started down the hill again.

I had not avoided the curious eyes. The people of the village stood in groups all around me as I entered with Kip straining forward on the leash. I knew they considered the white woman a strange spectacle. My skin was different, my hair was different, my dress was different—even my dog, leashed and fluffy, was different.

I smiled and softly greeted them in the Indian tongue. I was thankful that at least I knew their language.

No one answered my words or smiled in return. They continued to stare, moving back slightly from the path that led me to the small cabin.

Relieved, at last I reached my husband and hoped to be able to divert some of the staring eyes. I wished for a door to duck through, but there was only one in the very small cabin, where men were busy moving in and out, carrying crates and boxes.

"Well," said Wynn in a tired-sounding voice, "we are here." Then his tone turned teasing. "I thought for a minute that you got lost."

"I was in no hurry," I explained, and Wynn smiled, remembering the "hurry" I had been in throughout the morning.

"It isn't much, is it?" he said then, nodding his head at the cabin.

I tried to sound cheerful. "It'll do for now," I responded.

"What do you mean, for now? This is it, Elizabeth. This is our new home."

"It is?" I know that shock registered in my voice.

"It is. I'm sorry, Elizabeth. I had expected something better than this—even for here."

I had expected something better than this, too. Never had I thought that anyone lived in such crowded, miserable quarters. I'm sure my face turned pale, in spite of my healthy tan and my sun-burned nose.

I recovered as quickly as I could, gulped away the tears in the back of my throat, and tried to speak. My voice sounded strange, forced. "We'll manage," was all I could say.

"Why don't you find a spot in the shade some-where until the men are done unloading?" Wynn suggested, and I nodded dumbly and moved Kip around the cabin.

Indian cabins were all around us. There was no place to go where I wouldn't be subject to staring eyes. I wasn't ready for that yet. I wished I could go into the house to get away from it all, but I would only be in the way. Goodness knows, there was little room in there as it was.

With new determination I lifted my chin, took Kip's leash well in hand and started down the trail that led in a winding, circuitous route out of the village.

It took several minutes to walk far enough to be clear of the shabby little cabins. Kip whimpered and complained as I hurried him along. He wished to stop and investigate his new surroundings and make the acquaintance of the many thin, rough-coated dogs that strained against their tethers.

I hurried Kip right on by.

When we finally reached the woods beyond the village, I slowed my pace. I took a deep breath of the fresh summer air. It was tangy with the smell of pine trees and scented flowers. A small stream trickled nearby, and I followed the path that led along the bank.

We had not gone far when we came to a small lake. I looked out across it, enjoying its beauty, its tranquillity. I cannot explain what that little lake did for my spirits at that moment.

Here was a hallowed spot in the middle of all the squalor, the disappointment, of the little village. Here was someplace where I could go to refresh my soul. I eased myself down on the grass beside the waters and let my frustration and loneliness drain from me.

Surely, God is in this place. The words formed in my mind without any conscious effort. As I repeated them again, a quiet peacefulness settled upon me.

"Surely, God is in this place." I spoke the words aloud. It was true. It was a promise. It was enough.

Chapter Three

A New Home

The sun was dipping behind the western horizon and the evening was beginning to cool when I re-traced my steps down the path and into the village. The familiar scent of woodsmoke greeted me, and I breathed it in deeply. Maybe life in this new village wouldn't be so different after all.

For one panic-stricken moment I feared I might not be able to find the shabby little cabin that was to be our new home amid all the other shabby little cabins. But Kip led me right to it. Actually, I think I would have found it without difficulty, even by my-self. There simply was no other cabin in the village with so much activity. One wagon still stood in front of our little building, boxes and crates piled high in the wagon box. I wondered why Wynn had not in-structed the men to unload all the things.

I entered the door with caution, not sure just what I would find. In among boxes and empty crates, I found Wynn working alone and trying to sort some order out of the chaos. He looked up as I entered, relief showing in his eyes.

"I was a little worried about you," he said. "I wondered where you had gone, but one of the children said you took the path out of the village. If you hadn't come back soon, I would have been out looking for you."

"I'm sorry," I quickly apologized. "I didn't mean to alarm you. I just thought it would take some time until things were settled down so I could get in the cabin."

Wynn was quick to reassure me. "Well, I felt better knowing that you had Kip, and also knowing that you have a good sense of direction in the woods now. I was quite sure you wouldn't take yourself too far to find your way back again."

"I found a lake," I informed him with some excitement.

Wynn's head lifted from his hammering on the crate.

"I found a lake," I repeated. "It isn't very big, but it is lovely."

Wynn seemed to realize that the little lake was important to me.

"You'll have to show it to me," he stated with a brief smile.

"I will," I promised, "just as soon as we get settled."

I moved forward then, slipping Kip's leash so he was free to explore his new home. There wasn't much to explore. He would have it covered in two or three minutes. For me, it might take a little longer.

"I see there is still a lot to be unloaded," I remarked as I moved forward.

"I don't know what we'll do with it," responded Wynn doubtfully.

"What do you mean, 'do with it'?" I asked him.

"There's no storage available, and it will never fit in here. We might just have to throw a tarp over it and leave it on the wagon."

My eyes traveled over the cabin. Wynn was right. It was already very crowded. There was a blackened cookstove, a handmade table, two wooden chairs, a fireplace, a sagging bed in the corner, and a few rough wooden shelves. That was it.

Above me were dusty, weathered rafters. My first sight from the hill had been right. The roof did sag. I hoped it would not come crashing down upon us with the first heavy snowstorm.

My eyes turned then to the floor. It was hard-packed earth. Imagine! Not even rough boards to cover the dirt.

I had never lived in a dwelling with an earthen floor before. I wondered how I would manage living in one now. *At least it won't need washing*, I thought ruefully. I closed my eyes tightly as a shudder passed through me.

"We will soon need the lamp," Wynn was saying. "Do you remember what crate it was packed in?"

His words jolted me back to my senses. I tried to think. Yes, it was the big crate, the one with our bedding. I moved forward to point it out.

Wynn soon had the crate open and I joined him to remove the contents.

"I'll get this crate out of our way and make some more room," offered Wynn. "Perhaps with it out of the center of things, there will be enough room for you to make us some supper."

I looked toward the stove. Already a brisk fire was heating the room. The cooking surface was much smaller than I was used to. It looked like it would hold only the kettle and one pot at a time. I went over to check the kettle for water. It was already filled. A pail of water stood on the nearby shelf. It too had been filled with fresh water. *Dear Wynn*, I noted mentally. He was so thoughtful. I turned to find that food supplies had already been arranged on the two shelves provided. Our dishes were stacked on the small table.

"I don't know where you are going to find room to store things," said Wynn. "Those two shelves won't hold much."

Wynn was right. I looked around. There didn't seem to be any wall space left to build more shelves either.

"Some things can be hung up," I said, noticing a few nails in the walls.

With Wynn working to empty some boxes and clear some space, and me busy with our first meal, we began to feel that this small, poorly built cabin was going to be home.

When I had our supper ready, Wynn laid aside

his hammer and went outside to wash in the basin he had set on a stump by the door. Soon he was back, his sleeves still pushed up and his hairline wet from rinsing his face. He looked tired—and he hadn't even begun to unpack his office supplies or medicines.

"Where is your office?" I asked him after we had bowed in prayer together.

"There isn't one," he answered simply.

"Nothing?"

"Nope."

"What did the last Mountie do?"

"He was alone, so he just stacked things up by the wall, I guess."

"Oh," was all the answer I could manage.

"You're the first white woman to live in this village, Elizabeth," Wynn went on.

"I am?" Suddenly I felt a heavy responsibility. As the first one here, I had much to uphold. The people of the village would undoubtedly judge the whole white race by what they found in me. It was scary, in a way.

Would I be found worthy? Would I be able to contribute to their way of life, or would I appear to threaten it? Would I fit in where no white woman had been before? Would the Indian women feel free to come and sip tea, or would they see me a strange creature with odd ways who should be shunned and avoided?

I did not have the answer to any of those

questions. I looked at the small space around me. I knew without even visiting the other homes that this one was much like theirs. I smiled. I was beginning to feel some comfort in my strange, new home. If I lived like they lived, then surely it would not be as difficult for me to cross the barriers. If my floor was dirt, if my stove was small, if my bed stood in the corner of the same room, then wouldn't the Indian women find it easier to accept me as one of them?

Wynn must have noticed my smile. He lifted his head and looked at me, the question showing in his eyes.

"Well," I said, "I might be white, but my home will be no different. Perhaps that will make it easier to become one of them."

Wynn nodded. "Maybe so," he said slowly, "but I am sorry, Elizabeth, that it has to be so . . . so . . . uncomfortable for you."

I shrugged my shoulders. "Uncomfortable, yes. But it certainly isn't impossible, is it? I mean, with so many people living this way, I guess one must be able to do it and survive."

Wynn still looked doubtful. I was sure he was sorry he had agreed to bring me here.

"Look at it this way," I said, attempting to make my voice light. "Think of the little time that it will take to keep house. Why, I'll be able to loaf away hour after hour out by that little lake."

Wynn appreciated my effort, I know he did, but

he still wasn't quite ready to respond.

During the days that lay ahead, I would have to show him, bit by bit, that I was able to handle living in such a poor little cabin as a home. It would take time. First I would have to thoroughly convince myself.

A deep thankfulness swept through me that this was my second experience, not my first, in Wynn's wilderness. If I had faced such conditions when originally coming to the Northland, I was sure I would not have been able to accept it as readily. Now, bit by bit, I had been seasoned to the rigors of the North. I felt that I might even be ready to endure such stark barrenness. After all, it would not be for long. Wynn himself had said that the Force never left a man for too long in one location—perhaps not more than three or four years.

I looked about me. Three or four years seemed like an awfully long time.

Chapter Four

Getting Settled

The next few days were busy with unpacking, sorting and repacking anything not absolutely essential. There was no way that all our material goods, few as they were, would fit in our tiny cabin.

It was very difficult for me to decide what I could live without. I had thought I was already down to the basics in the two rooms, plus storeroom, plus office, that we had occupied at Beaver River. Looking about me now, our Beaver River cabin seemed like a large, spacious home in comparison.

Now I began to wish that Kip had been raised as an outside dog. He seemed to be underfoot no matter where I stepped.

I carefully sorted my pots and dishes, keeping only a minimum. If we should ever have company, I would need to wash plates and cutlery before I could serve them, but it was the only way I could make things fit. I allowed only one extra of each item, and packed all the serving dishes. I would dish up our meals directly from the stove. Two pots and a frying pan were hung on nails on the already crowded wall. I did not even have room to put up my pictures of Samuel, so carefully drawn by Wawasee. With a heavy heart, I packed them away in one of the crates to be stored.

My washtubs, brooms, dustpan, scrubboard, and anything else that would hang, were also on the wall. Back at Beaver River many of these things had hung on the outside of our cabin. Here, according to the trader who ran the post, everything had to be hung on the inside. The people of the village understood that anything outside was community property. Only they often forgot to bring the items back to the spot from which they had originally borrowed them.

I wondered about the possibility of adding on a room or two, but I didn't say anything to Wynn. He was busy enough trying to sort through his new responsibilities and figure out where to keep his much-needed supplies.

I had not realized how much I had enjoyed the ready water supply of our Beaver River well until we reached this new village. There was no handy well with a pump here. All our water had to be carried from the stream which was almost a quarter of a mile from the settlement. One soon learned to conserve. I found that one kettleful would do many jobs before it was thrown out to settle the dust on our path.

The other problem concerned the fact that there was no outbuilding. In Beaver River Wynn quickly had a building constructed for more privacy and convenience for me as his new bride. Here, there did not seem to be materials, labor, nor time for that construction. I had to quickly learn the "rule" of the villagers so I would know which paths were used by the women and children, and which paths to avoid. There were no signs with directional arrows—this was an unwritten understanding of village life.

When I felt I had packed away everything I could possibly do without, Wynn placed all the full boxes back on one of the wagons and carefully covered them with a canvas tarp to keep out the rain or snow. Then he tied heavy ropes backward and forward, over and under the wagon, to keep out other things. I hated those crisscrossed ropes. They seemed to speak of a way of life that was foreign and objectionable to me.

Wynn still had not found a place to keep his medical supplies, so he had to stack them in our cabin. Already every available space seemed to be filled with our few belongings. The extra blankets and our clothing were in boxes under our bed. Boxes of canned foods were stacked beneath the table. When we sat to eat a meal, we had to turn sideways in our chairs since our feet would not fit beneath our table.

There was room in the middle of our floor for the one bearskin rug. It helped to hide some of the earthen floor. I placed a few cushions on our bed. Seeing we had no couch of any kind, I felt it would be nice to have some extra back support, but in the days that followed I tired quickly of shifting the cushions each time we went to bed. I began to wish I had packed them away, too. But they did add a note of color and cheeriness to our drab surroundings, I decided.

More than a week had gone by before I visited the village trading post. There was no use buying anything more, since I couldn't find room even for what we had on hand. I went to the store more to make the acquaintance of the trader and the villagers than anything. I had been outside my own cabin very little in the few days I had been in the settlement. It was now time to meet the people and make some new friends.

English would do me no good in Smoke Lake. None of the people understood it. Even the trader in the store knew only a few English words. He spoke the Indian dialect like a native, which he actually was in part, though his mother tongue was French. I was thankful I had at least a working knowledge of the Indian tongue.

I met two women from the village as I walked to the trading post, and I smiled and greeted them in their own language. But they avoided eye contact and passed on, looking almost frightened. It was easy to see it would take some time for me, the white woman of the lawman, to be accepted. I would need to be patient.

I entered the store by its one low door and looked

around. The interior was dark and smelled strongly of furs and tobacco smoke—not a pleasant smell at the best of times, and in the close, suffocating little building, it was nearly unbearable. I held my breath against it and looked about. I did need eggs and lard, if they were to be had. In the clutter of the small store, I saw nothing that looked like egg crates or lard pails, but then not everything was visible, I reminded myself.

The trader eyed me shrewdly, squinting against the smoke wafting up from his hand-rolled cigarette and into his eyes. He spoke to me, but I did not understand a word of it.

"I'm sorry," I said in English, forgetting for a moment, "I don't understand."

He gave me a quizzical look and shrugged his shoulders.

I remembered then, and I switched over to the Indian tongue. He answered me in the native dialect, though his words were accented much differently than mine.

At least we can understand one another, I sighed in relief.

"I need eggs," I announced carefully, using the rather unfamiliar Indian words.

"No eggs," he informed me with an accompanying shake of the head.

"I also need some lard."

"No lard," he stated.

35

"Oh, my," I said in English. "What am I going to do now?"

"What you say?" he asked in the Indian dialect.

I looked at him apologetically and tried to explain that I had been speaking to myself.

"When in here," he informed me coldly in our mutual language, "best you speak to me—not you."

I had the feeling that I wasn't going to care too much for this surly man with his unkempt appearance and piercing eyes.

"You need coffee?" he asked me.

"No," I said, "no coffee. I have coffee now, thank you."

"You need flour?"

"No. No, I have flour."

"Sugar? Beans? Salt?"

I shook my head at each of the items as he listed them.

"Then why you come here?" he threw at me.

"I came for eggs and lard," I reminded him, just a bit annoyed.

"Don't got. Here we get eggs from bird nest, lard from animal. Not need eggs and lard in store."

I nodded again and headed for the door without even wishing him a good morning. Not surprising, he did not wish me a good morning either.

I was glad to again be in the fresh air. I breathed deeply of the scent of pine. Even the lazy smoke from the cabin fires could not disguise it.

I didn't wish to go back to my small, confined

cabin. Nothing there needed my further attention. My small house had been put in order, the pair of white curtains hung in the one small window, the rug spread upon the floor, the rest of the homey things packed away and stored on the wagon, and it would be hours before the bread dough would be ready for the oven. I was looking for companionship.

All around me people were busy with work and play. In front of the cabins women were weaving or sewing. Children played in the dirt or carried armloads of wood from the forest to the fires. Old men sat together in silent comradery. Young women chattered gayly as they spread pounded meat out to dry in the sun. But as soon as I approached, all fell silent. Eyes turned to the ground, tongues became hushed. My smile and my words in their language were totally ignored. They were not going to even give me a chance to get to know them.

In frustration and despair, I finally turned my steps toward our small cabin. If only I had Nimmie. If only there were an Anna or a Mrs. Sam to drop in for tea. I sighed deeply. I already could feel the loneliness of a long, silent winter closing in about me.

Kip met me at the door. His coat had now been restored to its usual fluffiness after the tangled mess it had become on the days spent on the trail. With washtub and brush I again had him looking like the house dog he had come to be. In comparison with the dogs of the village, he looked like he came from a different species entirely. I gave his head a pat, glad for his eager eyes and his waving tail.

At least here was a friendly face. I slipped on his leash and led him down the path that wove out of the village and along the stream to the quiet little lake. It might be that Kip would be the only companion I would have for the next few weeks—until I had somehow managed to break through the reserve of these villagers.

Chapter Five

Lonely Days

Our excursions to the small lake became almost a daily ritual for Kip and me. It was a beautiful walk and a lovely spot. No one seemed to resent us using the trail and sitting on the lakeshore or strolling through the pines, but no one seemed to pay much attention to us anyway. I still was unable to get the women to even acknowledge my presence. It was a very difficult time for me.

Wynn and I discussed it often at our supper table.

"Though these Indians are from the same tribe as our Beaver River Indians, they have not been exposed to the white man in the same way," he reminded me. "In coming to this remote village, it is as though we stepped back in time. We live with a very primitive people, Elizabeth."

Wynn sympathized with my need for friendship, but cautioned me to be patient and let the people have time to come to know and accept me. I secretly wondered just how long my patience would need to endure. I seemed to be getting nowhere.

Fall came with dry winds rustling the party-dressed leaves on the poplar trees and the birds twittering and instructing one another concerning their coming flight south. I loved the fall, but the thought of the coming winter, with no friends to help me see it through, concerned me. I needed to take action but I didn't know what to do.

Then one day I had an idea. I was passing down the path to again walk to the lake when I noticed two women enter the village with baskets of berries. So there *were* berries around! I did want some for the winter ahead. I also saw it as an opportunity to "build a bridge." Hadn't it been berries that had brought me my first friends at Beaver River? I hurried home to find some kind of container.

I left Kip behind in the cabin. I didn't want him to interfere in any way with my attempt to make friends. With a light step and heart, I went to find some village women.

I did not need to go far. Just down the trail from our cabin, two Indian women sat in the afternoon sun sewing buckskin moccasins. I approached them with my cooking pot extended and a smile on my lips.

As usual they stopped their chatter and lowered their eyes, but I was not to be discouraged so easily.

I greeted them with the proper Indian greeting. They did not return it as was the custom. I waited for a moment and when there was no response I raised the question.

"I want to pick berries," I informed them with my limited vocabulary.

Still no response. They continued their work, seeming nervous at my presence, but they did not look up nor acknowledge me.

"Where can I find berries?" I tried to keep my voice friendly in spite of how I was beginning to feel, but it wavered some.

One of the women grunted, and they both picked up their work and went into the cabin.

I could have cried. How was I ever going to make friends in this strange new village? I was about to turn around and go home again when I spotted two younger women, their babies on their backs, stirring a blackened pot over an open fire. Perhaps the younger ones would be less hostile, I decided, and headed for them.

They too dropped their eyes and ceased speaking when I came near, though their eyes did lift occasionally to steal little glances at me.

I greeted them, but did not wait for their response. I hastened right on. "I want to pick berries and I not know where they are. Can you tell me, please?"

For a moment there was silence and then they exchanged brief looks. One of them shrugged slightly, but the other pointed to the west and said simply, "There." It wasn't much, and it certainly didn't locate a patch for me, but it was the first word that had been spoken to me since I had entered their village. I smiled my thanks and started west.

I tramped around through the woods for the rest of the afternoon and still did not find a berry patch.

That night at our evening meal I told Wynn about my adventure of the day. He looked concerned, feeling my hurt at being rejected by this village, but we both acknowledged that it was a start—a small start.

"I've seen a patch or two as I've made my rounds," Wynn informed me. "Let's see if I can remember just where it was. Guess I didn't pay enough attention because I knew all your canning jars were packed away—even if we did get them out and fill them, we'd have no place to store them. If we put them back on the wagon, they'd just freeze with our first cold spell."

"Even if I just get a few for now, so that we can have some fresh and a pie or two," I said, realizing that Wynn was right about preserving, "it would be nice for a change."

Wynn nodded and took pencil and paper to draw me a crude little map.

The next morning I took Kip and my cooking pot, a sandwich for my lunch, and with Wynn's map in hand I set out to find a berry patch.

It took a bit of looking but I finally found a patch big enough to fill my pot, and I settled down to the picking, humming to myself as the pot slowly filled.

I let Kip run while I picked. He took little ventures into the woods, chasing rabbits and worrying the squirrels, but he returned often to keep check on me.

Midday I stopped for my sandwich. I wished I had a cup of tea to go with it. I was not far from the stream, so I left my pot and strolled to the stream for a drink. The water was cool and refreshing. I splashed a little on my face and washed the blue stain from my hands.

Kip lapped at the water, wading out in it just far enough to reach it with his tongue without bending too much. The flowing water licked at his legs and swirled around his nose as he thrust it into the stream.

I picked up a short stick and played a game of chase-the-stick with Kip for a few minutes. By the time our game was over, Kip was dripping wet from chasing the stick out into the middle of the stream. I forgot to keep my distance, and when Kip left the stream he shook water all over my skirt. I laughed at myself and ran back toward the berry patch and my nearly full pot.

Kip ran on ahead of me, still shaking wetness as he ran. He seemed to know exactly where we were going and led me directly toward my cooking pot with its berries. He reached it first—or would have reached it had he not suddenly stopped dead still, his hackles bristling and his throat rumbling.

His eyes were fastened on the spot where I had left my berries, and my eyes lifted from Kip to search out the pot as well.

There, feasting undeservedly from my hard-earned berries, was a skunk. I held my breath, not daring to stir.

The skunk seemed undisturbed. I wanted him to stay that way. I had no desire at all to tangle with him. I put a hand down to restrain Kip, but I wasn't fast enough.

Kip knew the berries were mine. He also knew that the skunk was an imposter. With his throat sending out warnings, he sprang forward to chase the skunk from the berry container.

It all happened so quickly I hardly had time to think. There was a flash as Kip left my side, the instant flag of the skunk's tail, a brief skirmish, and then Kip was screaming in rage and pain and rolling his head around in the debris on the forest floor as a sickening and powerful smell rolled over us.

I looked up from Kip just in time to see the last of the skunk disappearing through the underbrush.

I hurried Kip back to the stream. I didn't even need to throw in the stick for him to seek out the water. He plunged his whole head into its depths, burying himself in the coolness. His eyes stinging and his nose smarting, again and again he thrust his head into the stream.

It did nothing for the odor. It seemed to just grow worse and worse. I looked down at my skirt, then sniffed of my hands. Though I had not been sprayed directly by the skunk, I seemed to smell almost as bad as Kip. What in the world would I ever do now?

After Kip had received all the help he could get
from the flowing stream, we went back to the berry
patch to reclaim our pot.

I was tempted to leave it just where it sat. I
knew from the concentration of the smell in the area
that just to walk through the bushes and over the
ground would cover my shoes and skirts with more
of the offensive odor. Yet I couldn't afford to leave
the cooking pot behind. I had only one other with
which to cook.

I found a long stick and stretched as far as I
could to hook the pot and lift it to me. It slipped
from the pole mid-air and clattered to the ground.
Try as I might I could not get the handle hooked
again. I finally gave up and, hoisting my skirt the
best I could, waded through the short bushes and
reclaimed my pot. As I had anticipated, it reeked!

I emptied out the rest of the berries, nearly crying as I watched them fall into a small pile on the
ground, and headed once again for the stream. I
used sand to scrub and scour my pot, but even so
some of the smell seemed to cling to it. Whatever
would I do? I needed that cooking pot.

At last we started for home.

"Kip, you stink!" I informed him as I slipped his
leash back on, and then smiled in spite of myself—
the pot calling the kettle black. I was sure I was just
as offensive as the dog. And my cooking pot wasn't
much better.

I wondered just how in the world I would be able

to get back into the village without causing chaos.

"Well, at least they won't be able to ignore me," I said to Kip with a grin. But I really wasn't that amused by it all. We were in a terrible fix, and well I knew it. How in the world, and when in the world, would we ever be free of the odor?

Chapter Six

Blueberry Pie

The odor preceded us into the village. I heard children shouting the Indian word for skunk and then saw them run toward their cabins even before I came into the settlement. The women, too, left what they were doing and went indoors.

With a red face and a hurried step, I hastened toward my own cabin with the smelly Kip tightly in tow.

When we reached the cabin I tethered Kip outside and put my pot beside the door. Then I leaned down and removed my shoes, stepped just inside the door and removed my heavy skirt, reaching around the door to toss it back out onto the path. After that I removed the rest of my clothes and scrubbed with soap and water until I had my skin red and chafed. Still I smelled like a skunk!

I was forced to put clean garments on a still odorous body; then with a tub of hot sudsy water I attacked my clothes. I washed them as best as I could and hung them on my outside line. I could still smell them. I next took Kip and scrubbed him in the water. His wet fur seemed to smell worse, not better.

I saw many curious looks directed my way. Little clusters of Indian children stared without reservation, and the women gathered in whispery little groups, trying not to be as obvious as the children, but not succeeding very well.

I clamped my jaw and scrubbed harder on Kip. He whined and tried to pull away from me, but I scolded him mildly and scrubbed on. After all, he was the one who had gotten us into the mess!

In spite of all my efforts, when Wynn returned that night he was greeted by the strong smell of skunk.

"What do I do about it?" I moaned.

"Not much that you can do," Wynn answered.

"You mean nothing will help it?"

"Only time, as far as I know," responded Wynn.

I moaned again. "Time" always seemed so slow when you needed it to pass quickly.

"You could try filling the pot with dirt and burying your clothes," Wynn said. "Some seem to think that the earth takes some of the odor away."

"Kip is the worst," I insisted.

"Bury him, too, if you like," said Wynn, but he smiled to let me know he was teasing.

I did bury my clothes. I also buried the pot. The Indians watched me, hiding their eyes and their comments behind work-stained hands.

I did not leave my clothes buried for long. I could not take the chance of the moist ground causing rot.

The clothing I had was scarce enough at best and to lose an outfit simply would not do, even if I did reek each time I wore it. I dug it up carefully and washed it with soap and water again and hung it on the line.

The soil *did* seem to help my cooking pot. I scoured it thoroughly again and set it out in the sun.

Kip didn't seemed to mind being left outside— except at night. Then he would whine to come in. His whining wasn't as objectionable as his barking. He seemed to bark at every night sound. Wynn and I had supposed that we were used to the sound of barking dogs, but we found that Kip kept awakening us night after night with his fussing.

Undaunted, I was still determined to have a blueberry pie, so the next week I took Kip and again headed for the west and some berry patches. This time I did not remove Kip's leash when we got to the patch. Instead, I tied him to a small sapling and went about picking the berries to fill my pot.

Kip fussed and whined the whole time. To make it up to him, when I had picked my container full, I took him to the stream and let him loose so he could play in the water. We had a lively game of chase-the-stick. When I felt that he had had enough exercise, I slipped on his leash again, picked up my full pot of berries and headed for home.

The Indian people watched me enter the village again. I smiled and spoke to those who were near the path, but they turned their backs and pretended not to notice me. I tried not to let it bother me, but it did.

"Well, anyway," I said to Kip, who seemed to be the only one willing to listen to me, "I have my berries for pie."

When Wynn arrived home that night he was welcomed by a new aroma. The smell was nearly gone from Kip, my garments, and the cooking pot. Instead, the wonderful smell of fresh blueberry pie wafted throughout the cabin. I was pleased with myself. I had found the patch, I had persevered, I had baked my pie.

"Great!" said Wynn with an appreciative pat on my arm as he pushed back from the table after a second helping. His short, emphatic comment was enough to make it all worthwhile.

Chapter Seven

Winter

More determined than even my pursuit of berries was my search for new friends. Daily I took Kip for his walks, and each time I met or passed the Indian ladies I smiled and called out a greeting to them. They still chose to ignore me but even that did not stop me.

I made up my mind then to concentrate on the children. I was sure the children would be more responsive—after all, the children at Beaver River had learned to love both Kip and me.

I chose the paths where I heard children playing and smiled warmly and greeted them in their own tongue whenever I was near enough to be heard.

They lifted their heads and stared at me, but they refused to answer any of my questions. They did not even respond to the wild tail-wagging of Kip. They looked at us until their curiosity was satisfied, and then they either turned back to their play or else ran off, leaving us standing looking after them.

I even tried a little friendly "blackmail." I took some of my most colorful and fascinating books and held them out to them, showing them the pretty pictures as I let the pages flip slowly by. They stared at the strange new thing, but they did not draw closer or reach for it. In disappointment, I took my books and went back to my lonely cabin.

I stopped sharing my experiences with Wynn. It only pained him to hear of my loneliness. Instead I asked him all about his day. For the most part it was simply routine. He inspected boundaries, checked on trappers, distributed a small amount of medicine, settled a few local disputes, pulled a few teeth, delivered a few babies, and bandaged ever so many knife wounds, axe cuts, accidentally fish-hooked fingers, and sprained ankles.

I went to the trading post only when it was absolutely necessary. I did not feel comfortable with the dark-eyed trader, who watched me so closely as I looked around his crowded quarters trying to find the item I wanted.

He never moved from his spot behind his makeshift counter to assist me in any way. Squinting his eyes, puffing on his ever-present cigarette, he scowled at me as though I were an intruder rather than a customer.

Matches—or rather the lack of them—one day drove me from the safe confines of my cabin to the trading post. Wynn had asked me to get them, as our supply was low, and he would not be back from his patrol in time to visit the store.

I certainly couldn't tell Wynn I'd rather not go to

the post simply because I did not like the man, so I said nothing. Midmorning, I freshened up, closed the door on Kip and ventured forth.

On the path I again met women from the village. I smiled and nodded, giving the customary greeting. They would not look at me anyway.

I found the trading post the same as always, dark, stale and clouded with cigarette smoke. The trader stood behind his little barrier and scowled as two Indian women made their selections. I did not merit even a nod from any of them.

I stood back, patiently waiting until the women had finished their business and left by the low door. Then I quickly purchased the matches and left the store.

As I ducked out the door I heard voices just around the corner. The two Indian ladies were chatting. Surprised they had not already left the area, I stopped short. I knew they were right there on the path. I would need to pass by them. Would they answer me if I stopped and greeted them? I took a deep breath and determined to try it. And then some of their discussion reached me.

"Why she go there?"

"Don't know."

"Who?" A third woman must have joined them.

"The pale-faced one with the dog child."

The "dog child"? Why would they say that? Pale face, I could understand. It did not bother me to be referred to in such a way. But dog child? What did they ever mean by that?

And then I remembered Kip. The Indian women saw me often with Kip. They saw Kip fluffed and brushed. They had watched me bathe him and dry him with an old towel. They had seen me take him with me while others left their dogs tethered at home. They saw Kip enter our small cabin, while their dogs spent the days and nights, rain or shine, out-of-doors. They knew me to be a married woman, but they had never seen children at our home. The conclusion was that I had substituted a dog for the child I did not have.

Had I? Could the Indian women actually think that Kip, as much as I loved him, could take the place of the child I longed for? Never! If only they knew, I thought. If only they could understand my pain.

I turned and went around the trading post in the opposite direction so I would not need to confront the Indian women. It was a long detour, but I needed the long walk. I had to have time to think, to sort things out, to recover from the hurt.

I walked briskly while the tears streamed down my cheeks, praying as I walked. I had never thought it possible to be so lonely, so shut off from one's world.

At length I was able to get a firm hold on my emotions. I decided I would not engage in self-pity even though the days ahead did look bleak. *I have my Lord,* I told myself. *He has promised to be with me even to the end of the world.* For a few moments I felt that I must indeed be very near to the end of the world, my world, but I jacked up my courage and lifted my chin a little higher. God had promised He would never leave me nor forsake me. That held true on a city street, in a rural teacherage, or in a remote part of the North.

Besides, I had Wynn. Though his job took him away during the day and often into the night, still it was a comfort to know that he would be back and that he loved me and understood my needs and my longings.

And I had my "dog child." I smiled to myself. Kip might not be the companion I desired, but at least he was *someone*. I could talk to him, walk with him, and appreciate the fact that I was not entirely alone. Yes, I was thankful for Kip. It seemed he might be the only friend I would have in this settlement.

When I reached home, Kip met me at the door. His tongue teased at my hand and his curly tail waved a welcome flag. I patted his soft head.

"You won't understand a word of this," I said softly, "but in the village they think that you are my pampered 'child.' Well, you're not the child that I wanted, but at least you are a friend. Thanks for that. It looks like it might be just you and me here." I stopped to brush away some unbidden tears. "So—somehow we've got to make it on our own. It's not going to be easy—but I think we can do it."

Kip looked into my face and whined. He seemed to sense that I was troubled.

Then I made conscious effort to push the hurt from me so that I would be able to have a cheerful face for Wynn's return. I did not want him to be burdened with the pain I was feeling.

When Wynn entered our cabin I nodded toward the new supply of matches.

"Good," he said. "I was hoping you wouldn't forget. My supply pack is getting low, and I have a feeling that winter might be arriving any day now."

Wynn was right. In just two days' time, a north wind blew in a storm. It came howling around us with the wrath of the Indians' storm gods. In a few short hours, our settlement was covered with ten inches of snow.

From then on we lived with the cold and the wind. Each day more snow seemed to add to our discomfort. I kept busier now, and I guess that it was good for me. Bundled against the elements, I was constantly working just to keep our water supplied, our fires fed, and our clothes clean.

Kip and I still found time for walks—by the frozen stream to the frozen lake over frozen ground. I took the snowshoes and he plunged ahead breaking trail. We always came home refreshed from our outing and ready to stretch out before the open fire and let its warmth thaw our frost-stung bodies.

At night, when the supper was cleared away and Wynn sat at the crowded little table to do reports, I pestered him with all of the details of his day. He never rebuked me for my chatter—indeed, he encouraged it. Perhaps he knew he was the only one I had to talk to. At any rate, I enjoyed hearing each detail and felt that at least in a secondhand way I was getting acquainted with some of the area residents through Wynn.

Christmas came and went. I determined that I would not be lonely—well, lonely maybe, but not homesick. Homesickness was a miserable feeling and profited nothing.

And so, by taking one day at a time, I was managing to get through the long winter days. With the spring would come new activities. I would find some way to have a small garden and Kip and I would continue our exploration of the countryside. Perhaps I would even be able to take a trip or two with Wynn. Until then I would be patient, keep myself as busy as possible, and endeavor to keep my spirits up. As I had it figured, there would be only three more such years—at the most.

Chapter Eight

Neighbors

Our Indian neighbors enjoyed much more social life than the people in Beaver River had. Though we were never asked to participate, we often heard the beating of the drums as one ceremony or another was conducted. Toward the east end of the settlement there was a long, low building known as the council house where most of the ceremonies took place. The rest of them were held in the village "open."

At first the strange drumbeats and the rising and falling chants wafting over the night stillness seemed eery. The sounds reminded me that we were the outsiders here. We were in the midst of a different culture from our own. To us, the chants and drumbeats were distracting noise, but to the Indians these symbolized their religion, their very being. They believed in the "magic" and supernatural power of the chants and dances.

As far as we knew, the Indians in this remote yet rather large village had never seen a Christian missionary nor been introduced to his God. The old ways were never questioned and were held to with strict rigidity. The rain fell or the killing frost descended in accordance with the pleasure of the spirits, so it behooved the people to do all in their power to keep those gods happy with age-old ritual and age-old worship.

The drum beating and the dancing were performed to welcome the spring rain, to strengthen the spring calves of the moose and deer, to make quick and strong the trap, to thicken the pelts, to send the schools of fish, to make healthy the newborn, to safeguard the hunter, to protect the women, to give an easy "departure" to the elderly, and on and on.

It was no wonder, as the Indians felt obligated to perform all the rituals, that it seemed as if the drums were always beating, the rhythm of dancing feet always thrumming on the ground, the drone of chanting voices always rippling out over the frosty night air.

A death was a very important event to the villagers. Day and night they beat their drums and chanted as mourners wailed before their gods, impressing them with the fact that the soul departed would be greatly missed here on earth and thus should be equally welcomed into the new land.

The higher one was in the tribal caste system, the longer they would beat the drums. When the next-in-line as chieftain, the chief's eldest son, died in a drowning accident, the drumbeat continued for a total of seven days. For the chief himself, it would be just seven days plus one.

By the time the seven days had passed, my whole body was protesting. Kip and I took to the woods whenever we could, but even many miles from the village the drumming could still be heard in the cool, clear fall air.

When the ceremony finally did cease, I felt I had suddenly gone deaf. The world seemed a little shaky without the vibration of the shuffling feet. It was two days before I felt normal again.

The tribe had many superstitions and they held to them rigidly. It was not unusual to see a woman suddenly drop what she was carrying and run shrieking to her cabin to shut herself in behind closed doors because she had seen something "taboo."

Children, too, were very conscious of tribal customs and teachings. You could see them watching the sky, the woods, the ground for "signs" to live by.

So I should not have been surprised when word filtered back to me of the Indian women's fear that association with the "pale-faced" woman might somehow bring down the wrath of the gods. There didn't seem to be any consensus as to why the spirits might object, but the elders informed the younger, and the younger warned their children, and the villagers, with one accord, were afraid to test the conviction.

I could think of nothing I could do to break the

barrier—except wait. Surely if I continued to live among them, greet them in a friendly manner and not push in where I was not invited, in time they would see and understand that I did not invoke the anger of their gods.

The Indian people of this tribe had a strange conception concerning the rule of the Mountie. To them he represented the enforcement of the law. Law was closely tied to payment for sins committed. The gods frowned upon wrongdoing and reacted with a vengeance when one stepped out of line. Therefore, in some strange, invisible way, the white lawman might have some connections with the super powers. They treated Wynn with both deference and fear.

As Wynn's wife, I was suspect. Perhaps I had been brought to the village for the sole purpose of spying on the villagers, and as such I would report any misdeed to Wynn the moment he returned at the end of the day. Therefore no one wished to take any chances by having communication with the "pale-face."

The fact that I had no children and was often seen walking a dog made me even more suspect, and set me even further apart from the women of the village. I did wish I could do something about my circumstances, but I had no idea how I might break through the superstitions.

When I eventually had come to understand the reason for the shunning, I believe it did help my peace of mind. At least I did not feel rejected on a personal level. I prayed about it and left the entire matter in God's hands, in the meantime asking Him for patience and understanding.

I had to recognize also that my position as a white woman contrasted greatly with that of the Indian women. In their culture the women did most of the manual labor. The men hunted for the food, trapped the animals for fur and went to war if necessary. The woman, a laborer, was also in total subjection to the man, and her very posture showed her position. Never was she to stand before a man in the same way that another man would. Always her eyes were to be downcast and her attitude one of humility and respect.

Though very deeply committed to their religion, the Indian tribe was also dedicated to fun. They loved their ceremonies simply because they brought pleasure to an otherwise rather drab and difficult life. They celebrated births and weddings with gay abandon. They loved sporting events as well, wrestling and running and hunting, and the young men were very serious in their desire to better their opponents.

The young women loved the contests too. They stayed apart in shy, clustering groups, hiding their downcast dark eyes discretely behind slim, brown hands, but they never missed a thing. And though the young braves pretended that their skills were displayed for the eyes of the other men only, no one was fooled for a moment.

Many a marriage took place soon after one of their sporting events, with the winner making his intentions known to some young maiden of his choice by presenting her with gifts. If she accepted the gifts, it was understood that she accepted his proposal too.

The Indians were great practical jokers as well— particularly the young men, though the children too enjoyed playing pranks on one another. A young brave seemed to enjoy nothing better than to "bring down" another young fellow in the eyes of many witnesses. The laughter and teasing made the unfortunate hide his scarlet face in embarrassment. However, he usually got even at some future time when the prankster was least expecting it.

So we lived with our new neighbors—together, yet apart; inhabiting the same village, but feeling ourselves to be of another time and another world. It was so different from Beaver River, where we had been not only neighbors but true friends, sharing totally in the village life. Daily I prayed that somehow the reserve might be broken; that we would be seen as more than a "law-enforcer" and his "spying" wife; that the Indians might realize we had come as friends as well.

Chapter Nine

Spring

We dared to hope that spring was on the way when the sun began to spend more time in the sky and the days began to grow longer and warmer.

For Wynn, the winter had been uneventful. There were no major epidemics within the village, no disasters, and very few troublesome incidents.

For this we were truly thankful, for we weren't sure what the response of the people would have been if some calamity had fallen on the tribe soon after our arrival. Perhaps with their superstitious leanings they would have felt that the disaster had come because of us.

On one of the first warm days, Wynn suggested that I might like to go on an outing with him. I wholeheartedly agreed. It seemed forever since I had been beyond the exercise trails where I walked Kip.

I bundled up, for the temperature was still cool, and put the leash on Kip until we got beyond the settlement. The trip would not be long, so Wynn decided to dispense with the sled dogs. That way we could walk together and enjoy the signs of spring.

"If you want to pack a lunch, we'll celebrate the departure of another long winter," Wynn had said, so I prepared a picnic. Like the Indians, I was ready to celebrate almost anything.

There was enough winter snow left for us to lace on our snowshoes.

Kip was excited. He could sense this was a special outing when we were being joined by Wynn.

Wynn walked slower than his normal pace in order to accommodate me. I still had not become truly adept on snowshoes. Besides, I wished to enjoy every minute of the day. As we walked, I was full of my usual questions about everything from squirrels to ferns. Wynn pointed out trappers' boundaries and told me the names of some of our neighbors.

"Do you think they'll ever accept us?" I asked him. "I mean, as part of them, not as the 'Force'?"

"I don't know, Elizabeth. They don't seem to know much about the white man here. They don't have anything to base their trust on, as yet."

"But wasn't there a Mountie here before us?"

"Yes . . ." Wynn hesitated. "That might be some of the problem."

I looked at Wynn, concern showing in my eyes. "You mean they had a 'bad' officer?"

"No, not bad. He did his duty as the King's representative honestly enough. But he held himself apart from the people. From what I have heard, he might have even taken advantage of their belief that he might be . . . ah . . . different. If they wanted to think he was in cahoots with the spirits, then that was fine with him."

"Oh, Wynn! Surely he wouldn't—"

"Oh, he didn't foster it, I don't mean that, but he didn't mind if the Indian people thought him a little different—a little above them."

"But why?"

"It's hard to say. Some men just like having authority. He was a loner and didn't like to be bothered. One way to keep the villagers at a distance was to keep them believing that there was a 'great gulf' between them and the lawman, so to speak."

"I think that's terrible!" I blurted out. "And now we, who would like to befriend them and help them, have to bear the brunt of it all."

"We'll just have to keep chipping away at it. I think I am feeling a little less tension on the part of some of the men."

"I'm glad *someone* is making headway." I shook my head. "I sure haven't. This has been about the longest winter I ever remember—at least since the one when I had both the measles and the chicken pox as a child."

Wynn chuckled and hugged me.

We trudged on for a few moments in silence, both busy with our own thoughts. The brightness made me squint against the morning glare, and the snow squeaked with a delightful, clean sound as our snowshoes made crisscross tracks across the unbroken whiteness.

A bush rabbit streaked across the hill in front of us, and Kip was off on the chase. I could have told him not to bother. There was no way he was going to catch that rabbit. But I said nothing. Let him have his fun!

"You didn't tell me where we are going," I commented to Wynn.

"Oh, didn't I? There's a trapper out here who was burned when some of his clothing caught on fire—he fell asleep too close to his campfire coals. I thought I'd better check him out to see if he needs any attention."

"Was he badly burned?"

"I don't think so, but best not to take chances with infection. Some of these wounds aren't cleansed too carefully. An infection could give him more trouble than the original burn."

We found the cabin with no difficulty. I sat on a tree stump and waited while Wynn went to check on the man. When he came out, he said the injury fortunately wasn't deep, and the man had seemed to care for it properly. The burn was on his left leg, from his knee nearly down to the ankle. Wynn left him some medicated ointment and promised to stop by to see him in a couple days.

We retraced our steps to the brow of a hill and sat down on a log to eat our sandwiches. How good they tasted in the fresh air, especially after our exercise of the morning.

The sun climbed into the sky and sent down such warm rays that we both removed our heavy jackets.

"Do you think it is *really* spring?" I asked with great longing.

"Why not?" responded Wynn. "It's that time of year."

"I'm always afraid to hope for fear it will storm again," I confided.

"It might," Wynn replied, "but even that won't keep spring from coming. Slow it down a bit maybe, but spring will still come."

It was a good thought. Springtime and harvest, God had promised, will always come to the earth.

I breathed more deeply.

"I'm glad," I responded happily. "Glad that winter is almost over. Glad that I won't have to melt snow for water. I'd rather carry it by the pail from the stream. I'm glad that I'll be able to let the fires go out for part of the day. And I'm especially glad that I will be able to hang the laundry outside again—all of it. I am so tired of dodging under shirts and dresses and of having to move socks from bedpost to chair to bedpost." I sighed a deep sigh. "I really will be glad to see spring."

Wynn reached out and stroked my hair.

I broke the silent moment by turning to him. "Wynn, we haven't found a garden spot yet."

He smiled his slow, easy smile.

"No—guess we haven't."

"Well, we need to pick one."

"Guess there is plenty of time. You won't be planting for a few days yet, Elizabeth."

"I know, but we need to find a good one before—"

"There is all of the woods and all of the meadow. You can take your pick," he answered. "From what I hear, you'll be the only one in the whole area in need of one."

"It's a shame," I said, "that's what it is. All this beautiful soil—just going to waste."

Wynn looked around us at the heavy stand of trees. Under the snow we knew that grasses and plants grew in abundance.

"Well, not exactly to waste. All the forest creatures seem to feed very well."

"You know what I mean. It could be supplying nourishment for the people of the settlement."

"I guess it's doing that, too," said Wynn. "La-Meche tells me that they eat very well from the land."

At the name of the trader my back straightened somewhat. I still didn't feel comfortable with the man.

"Wynn," I asked, "do you know anything about him?"

"Who?"

"LaMeche. He seems so strange. So . . . so . . . sullen." I thought that my choice of word may be a compliment to the man, but I didn't want to do him an injustice.

"Louis LaMeche? Not much. His father was French and his mother Indian. His father moved into the area east of here about forty years ago and staked out a claim. He did well as a trapper until an epidemic hit. Both of the parents and all of the children were ill, though LaMeche seemed to make out the best. LeMeche was nine or so at the time. He struck out on his own to find help for his family. He got lost and it took him several days to find his way to a cabin. Even then he stumbled across it accidentally. By the time help got back to his cabin all his family were dead."

It was a dreadful story. My original assessment of the man needed altering. No wonder he was withdrawn and—and sullen. What an awful experience for a young boy to endure.

"What did he do then?" I found myself asking.

"Some of the local trappers got together and scraped up enough money to send him 'out.' Supposedly he had an aunt or someone near Winnipeg. He stayed for a few years, but he didn't like it, so he ended up coming back. He started the post about ten years ago. Been here ever since."

"Who told you all this?" I asked Wynn, wondering if LaMeche himself had shared it.

"It's in the files. It's not marked confidential—still, I don't think it's for common knowledge. Just thought that it might help you to understand the man a bit."

It certainly did. Now I was ashamed of myself for the way I had felt about Mr. LaMeche.

Wynn stood to his feet. "We'd better be getting on home," he stated. "I need to write up the report on Red Fox."

I stood too. I didn't want to return to the village. I disliked even more the thought of returning to the small cabin. I was so thankful that it would soon be spring again and I could enjoy more and more of the outdoors.

"Thanks for taking me along," I smiled at Wynn with deep appreciation. "I needed that."

Wynn reached out and took my hand.

"I needed it, too," he said. "I wish I could include you more often, Elizabeth. You're great company."

"Why, thank you, Sergeant Delaney," I teased. "Now that spring is here, I'll see if I can fit you into my crowded calendar again some time."

Wynn gave me a wink and a smile, and we headed for home.

Chapter Ten

Planting the Seed

"I think it's time."

I had been waiting for those words from Wynn for *ages*! When he spoke them now I could hardly refrain from cheering. Instead I smothered my enthusiasm by nearly smothering Wynn.

He laughed as I hugged him. "If you don't leave me a little breath!" he gasped, "I won't be able to help you."

Then he hugged me in return before I quickly pulled away and began scurrying around in preparation.

It was gardening time! That meant the long winter was over. That meant I could again be outside more. That meant our poor diet could be supplemented with fresh vegetables. I could hardly wait!

"Have you picked a spot?" Wynn asked me.

"Sort of. It has to be in the open. We have no way to clear trees and, anyway, it seems that it would grow much better out where it could get plenty of sun."

Wynn nodded in agreement.

"There's that small clearing to the south of the village, but the children use it a lot. Then there is the little meadow to the west. Kip and I go there often. It is pretty, but I'm afraid it might be a little low and wet."

Wynn was following every word I spoke.

"Then there is a large meadow to the east, but the men run their horses in there. The lake has some nice areas around it, but I don't think the deer and moose would leave it alone."

I stopped for a quick breath.

"So—I have decided that the best spot I've seen so far is that little clearing down at the stream. The water forks there and leaves a little island right out in the middle. You have to get to it by the use of those steppingstones, though when the water is high they are under water and you have to go upstream a ways and use a fallen log. Have you seen it? It looks like a cabin might have stood there at one time."

I was almost out of breath by the time I finished, but I was rewarded by a wide grin from Wynn.

"Good scouting, Elizabeth." He gave me a playful pat on the bottom. "Your eyes are as sharp as an Indian's. Good choice. Lead the way."

So carrying my basket of beloved seed, and Wynn with a shovel over his shoulder, and Kip bounding along beside us to oversee the project, we started that spring Saturday morning by heading down the winding path leading to the small stream.

There were many curious eyes following our passing, you can be sure. *They must be wondering whom we are planning to bury, seeing Wynn with his shovel*, I thought, and I couldn't help but be amused.

When we reached the place I had selected, Wynn went right to work. It wasn't easy digging. The ground was heavy with wild grasses and plants. I had been right. A cabin had stood there at one time. We found bits and pieces of the debris as Wynn dug.

I helped to shake the dirt from the clods as Wynn turned them over. The soil was rich and promising, and it felt so good to allow it to sift through my fingers. Already I was tasting carrots and potatoes.

"Oh, oh!" Wynn exclaimed as he turned over a shovelful of ground with some strange objects intertwined in it.

"What is it?" I asked, wondering why he stopped to study the items.

Wynn turned them over with one hand, looking at each one carefully.

"We might have done it again, Elizabeth," he said. "These are some objects used by a medicine man."

I couldn't follow Wynn's reasoning. I shook my head in perplexity. "So?"

"I don't know how this cabin burned, or who this fellow was, but I've a feeling that we should find out before we go any further," went on Wynn.

"Are you saying that . . . that . . . ?"

"I'm saying that this spot might be another of their taboos."

"Oh—h!" escaped my lips in a soft, pleading whisper. Surely I hadn't done something more to separate us from the village people.

"What should we do?" I asked Wynn, my face draining of its color.

"I'm not sure. Guess I'll go see LaMeche. We've already disturbed the place. I'd better see how much fuss it might cause."

"Should I go with you?" I asked in a nervous voice, thinking that after all it was my fault and I should be there to shoulder the blame and excuse Wynn.

"No. No need for that. You can wait here. I shouldn't be long."

So saying, Wynn thrust his shovel into the soil and started up the path to the village.

I sat down in the grass, my eyes on the shovelful of evidence, nervous and agitated. I don't know what I expected might happen, but I was afraid that *something* might. Would the Indians burn down our cabin in order to avenge the disturbance of their beloved medicine man?

I decided to move farther away. I found a fallen log a few feet away in the shade of a small clump of poplar trees growing on the little island, and settled myself on it.

The minutes seemed to drag by, but in reality it wasn't long until Wynn was back. I stood to my feet when I saw him coming, but when he arrived he motioned me back to the seat on the log and sat down beside me.

"It was a medicine man who lived in the cabin, all right—but he wasn't a popular one with the villagers. In fact, he moved in from another area and took over the position of the local witch doctor by force—or by stronger "medicine." There almost was a local war over it. He brought several of his followers with him, and they settled over toward that large meadow." Wynn pointed off to the meadow.

"An epidemic of some kind hit the outside camp," he went on. "The villagers said it was due to the 'medicine' of the rightful, resident chief, who was also the village witch doctor. They said that the gods were showing who really was the man who should have power in the village.

"The intruding medicine man also got sick and died with the fever. Some daring young braves, in an act of defiance and revenge, rode out and burned his cabin, with his body in it. Those of his people who survived the disease hurriedly moved on. Then the villagers had a great victory celebration. Since that time, no one has ever visited the island. We were right—it is taboo."

"Oh, dear," was all I could say.

"Look at it this way, Elizabeth," Wynn said with a grin, "you'll never need to fear having raiders in your garden."

"Oh, Wynn!" I exclaimed, horrified that he should joke about it.

Wynn stood to his feet, still laughing at his comment, walked over to reclaim his shovel, and thrust it deeply into the earth, turning over another shovelful of the rich soil and a few more Indian relics.

"What are you doing?" I gasped.

"I'm digging you a garden."

"But—"

"Any harm we are going to do has already been done. We might as well enjoy the garden spot."

"Are you sure?" I was still hesitant.

"I'm sure. The Indians leave this spot alone because they are afraid of it—not because they hold it sacred."

I thought about that. Certainly I was not afraid of this bit of ground, even if a medicine man had lived upon it. It was, after all, God's creation and God's bit of land. If He chose to grant me a good garden here, then I would accept it as from His hand. I went to join Wynn.

We spent the rest of the morning preparing the soil. Often we felt hidden eyes watching us from among the trees at the other side of the stream. We tried not to let it bother us and went right on with our digging. "See," I wanted to shout to them, "there is no curse on this ground. The power of the medicine man does not compare to the power of the One True God who created this soil and planted these grasses." But I said nothing. I prayed that time might prove it to the people.

In the meantime, I truly was sorry we inadvertently had placed another barrier between the people and ourselves. We so much wanted to help them, to live with them, to be their friends, but we could not because of all of their religious taboos.

By the time the soil was tilled, the sun was high in the sky. I fell to my knees as Wynn dug little trenches for me to place the seeds. I rejoiced as each seed dropped in and I patted the rich, brown soil over them. I could hardly wait for them to grow.

Wynn broke into my reverie.

"I had thought that we would need to build a makeshift fence. That is the customary sign to the villagers that this spot has ownership and should not be disturbed, but I guess it won't be needed out here, under the circumstances."

"Oh, Wynn," I moaned. "I do hope I haven't gotten you into any trouble."

"We didn't do it intentionally, Elizabeth," Wynn said, straightening and placing a hand on his back. It had been hard work. "Who knows, God might use it for good."

"Oh, I hope so." It was almost a prayer.

"I've been thinking," Wynn went on, "maybe I should move the sled dogs out here. It would save me paying rent for that little space from LaMeche and would give them so much more room. Right now I have to have their tethers so short they hardly have room to move around. I could stake them all around your garden. There's plenty of room and it would keep the animals from raiding."

It sounded like a good idea to me. I wasn't opposed at all to sharing my island with Wynn's dogs.

"Don't forget to leave me lots of clearance for my path," I warned him. "I don't trust some of your dogs."

Wynn laughed, then went on. "There's only one problem."

"What?"

"Kip."

"Kip? How is he a problem?" I puzzled.

"You couldn't let him run free when you come to the garden. He'd get himself into a fight every time."

I knew Wynn was right.

"I'll just have to keep him leashed, too, when we are here," I said. "He can get his exercise elsewhere."

I patted the soil over the last seeds and stood up. Our garden was done. Now I just had to wait and watch. Mother Nature, God's "force," would do the rest.

Chapter Eleven

Introductions

With the warm days of spring, the mosquitoes came in droves and the blackflies too began to hatch and torment us. I draped cloth down the back of my neck whenever I went to the stream for water, to work in my garden or to exercise Kip. Even so I was bitten unmercifully every time I left the small cabin.

Those little creatures weren't enough to keep me in, however. I was out as much as I could dream up reasons to be. I had been confined in the few feet of cabin space long enough over the dreary winter.

I even found reasons to go to the store. Now that I knew something about the trader, I tried to be more patient and understanding. I will admit it was difficult. He was still sour and unfriendly. He snapped when spoken to, and blew his cigarette smoke in my face whenever I came near his counter to settle my account. I tried not to let it bother me, but sometimes it was hard to keep my smile in place.

I still spoke to the Indian women each time I had contact with them. I don't know if it was just wishful thinking, but I was beginning to feel that they didn't turn from me quite as quickly as they had at first. Perhaps they were getting used to my imposing myself upon them.

The little children could not be accused of being friendly toward me, but they didn't scatter quite as quickly either. Sometimes they didn't even run, just stared for a moment and then returned to their play.

I could hardly call it a triumph, but with the sun overhead and my garden sending up little spikes of promise, I couldn't help but feel a happiness in my heart.

Wynn had moved his dogs to the island and whenever I went to weed, I also carried food scraps I had gathered to feed his dogs. They were beginning to welcome me with little yips of anticipation, and I enjoyed being wanted—even by sled dogs. I found that some of them enjoyed petting, and I ventured close enough to do that. They really weren't such a bad lot after all, if you took them one by one.

My favorite was Flash, the lead dog, a full-blooded brother of Kip. Though Flash was not as pretty as Kip, he certainly was an impressive dog. His shoulders were thickset, his legs muscled and strong, his face intelligent, and his eyes deep blue and trusting. I petted Flash more than any of the others and we soon became close friends.

I wished there were a way to get the two brother dogs together. Surely they would realize they were kin and lay aside all challenges for supremacy, but when I mentioned the idea to Wynn, he laughed.

"Don't you believe it for a minute, Elizabeth," he warned me. "Kip and Flash are both determined to be top dog. Neither of them would give an inch. You'd have the worst fight on your hands you've ever seen."

Well, I had seen enough dog fights since coming to the North that I certainly didn't want to see a "worse" one, so I kept Kip well away from his brother.

I felt a bit guilty about making friends with Wynn's dogs. I wasn't sure how a sled dog was to be treated. I knew that many of the trappers handled theirs with a heavy hand and no mercy or love whatever. I knew Wynn did not treat his dogs in that manner, but just how *did* he handle his dogs? Could I spoil them with my petting and pampering? I decided I had better check with Wynn.

One night at our evening meal, I raised the subject.

"When I go out to the garden, I take food scraps to your dogs."

I watched for Wynn's reaction. No frown appeared.

I went on. "They really aren't so bad."

" 'Course not," said Wynn. "I don't know why you were afraid of them in the first place."

"Well, I didn't know them really. I still don't know all of their names."

I wanted to ask Wynn if I would spoil them by

petting them, but Wynn stood to his feet.

"How about if I take you out and introduce you?" said Wynn. "If you leave the dishes, we still have time before dark."

Wynn knew I seldom left unwashed dishes, but this time I agreed.

"Okay," I nodded. "You've got yourself a date. I've been aching to show you how quickly the garden is growing. You just wouldn't believe it! Medicine man or no, I still think we picked the best spot in the whole region for our garden."

Wynn chuckled and picked up his plate and cup and carried it to the dishpan. I followed behind him and in next to no time our table was cleared, and I was ready to go.

I had thought that the dogs welcomed me when I came to the island, and so they did; but you should have heard the din when they saw Wynn! Each dog clammered for his attention, and he made the rounds, ruffling fluffy fur and petting bodies that wiggled from head to tail as they squirmed in their eagerness to get some of the loving. I stood amazed. I would never worry about spoiling Wynn's sled dogs again.

"This is Flash," Wynn said, burying his face against the thick fur of the dog's coat as he murmured strange sounds that only he and the dog understood.

I knew Flash.

"He's the best lead dog in the whole north country," Wynn went on. "I'd put him up against any other—any day. He sleeps right beside me when we are on the trail. I never tether him. Nothing would get near me without Flash warning me."

I didn't know that before. I was comforted to know that Wynn had Flash on "guard duty." I felt a new appreciation for the team leader. I reached down and patted his massive head.

We moved on.

"This is Peewee," said Wynn, "the only dog in the bunch that Flash has not whipped into submission. He hasn't needed to. Peewee has never questioned his authority. Peewee is small, but all heart and willpower. He'd never give up while he had an ounce of energy left."

Wynn knelt down and took the dog's head in his hands. The dog whined, deep devotion written all over him.

"Peewee would do anything I asked of him," said Wynn, "or die trying. Great little dog, aren't you, Peewee?"

I felt a lump in my throat as I looked at the small animal. In my mind's eye I had visions of this little fellow valiantly struggling to pull his share of the load. He was smaller than the usual sled dogs, but if Wynn could boast of him in this manner, then I knew he was worthy to be harnessed next to the great Flash.

"This is Tip. How are you, Tippy?" Wynn ruffled the dog's fur and played with her ears. "She loves to be praised, hates to be scolded. Temperamental, just like any woman—make that *many* women." Wynn stopped long enough to laugh at his own remark and stroke Tip's dark brown fur.

"Here's Keenoo. He's a half brother of Flash. Notice some of the same markings. He's the heaviest dog of the team. I count on him when I have a heavy load. Boy, can he pull! Might even be able to outpull Flash—though I've never tested it. But Flash is the more intelligent of the two. In spite of his size, Keenoo hates to fight. Uncommon for his breed."

Wynn stopped to pet the dog, who pushed up against him, thrusting his nose deeply into Wynn's hand.

"And this is Franco. I wouldn't get too close to him. He's the least friendly of the lot. He'll let me pet him if I don't overdo it, but he doesn't take to others very quickly."

Franco growled deeply within his throat as his eyes held my face, then he turned to Wynn and his tail waved, ever so slightly.

Wynn patted and talked to him, just as he had each dog, and then we moved on again.

"Why do you keep him?" I asked, concerned about the difference in that last dog's temperament.

"He's a good worker," said Wynn, "and he's never been a problem. He's the quickest to pick a fight and Flash has to straighten him out every so often, but he settles down and does his job when he has to."

I turned to get another look at Franco, and found

his sharp eyes still upon me. It was a bit unnerving. I wondered if he was jealous of me being with Wynn.

"He sure seems to have a chip on his shoulder," I commented.

"That's a good way to describe him," Wynn laughed. "He certainly does seem to have a chip on his shoulder."

There were two more dogs to go. They whined and pulled at their tethers, anxious for Wynn to get to them.

"This is Morley. He's sort of ordinary, I guess, but he works well and he tries hard, don't you, Morley? He has unusually sensitive ears. Morley is usually the first one to alert me if something or someone is in the area. Sometimes he is too quick. He growls over a mouse visiting a grass clump fifty feet away."

I knew Wynn was purposely exaggerating, but we both laughed.

"Hard to get your sleep sometimes, with Morley near you on the trail," went on Wynn, "but once or twice I've been thankful for his keen sense of hearing."

Wynn stopped to pamper Morley.

"And last of all, this is Revva, the other female. I'm thinking of using her to raise me some pups. With her as a mother and Flash to father them, I think I could get some top-notch sled dogs. Look at her intelligent eyes and her broad head. See the thick shoulders and deep chest. She has a great deal of stamina on the trail—something very important for a sled dog. I hate to lose her from the team, but I think she would be of even more value to me raising puppies."

Wynn leaned down to run a hand over Revva's silky side. She pushed up against him, begging for more attention. I leaned to pet her, too. She licked at my hand, letting me know she welcomed my caresses.

"So now you know them all," Wynn said, still stroking Revva as he spoke. "The only one you shouldn't get too close to is Franco. Leave him alone—at least for the present."

I nodded. I certainly would not be pushing Franco, yet deep inside me was a desire to win the friendship even of that unfriendly dog. I would take it slow and easy, but I knew I would try.

"I've already been petting Flash and Peewee and Revva," I admitted, rather hesitantly.

"Good," said Wynn. "They like lots of love and attention."

I let out my breath. So I hadn't done anything wrong in babying his dogs. Dogs, like people, needed lots of assurance that they were loved and appreciated. Wynn knew that. He treated them that way as well.

I leaned over to give Revva one last pat. The sun had left us. The twilight seeped in around us, cloaking us in a comfortable garment of softness. The evening sounds began to fill the air. Off in the forest a bull moose called out a challenge, or a love call, I did not know which. A screech owl sounded an alarm to our right. In the distance a wolf lifted its nose skyward and poured out his melancholy into a long, penetrating, lonely call. Revva shivered beneath my hand.

"She's not afraid of a wolf, is she?" I asked Wynn. I knew that I shivered even yet whenever I heard one of them.

"No," said Wynn. "I don't think it's fear. She is too closely related to that wolf out there to be afraid of him. Perhaps it's just the 'wild' in her that is responding."

I stroked the dog. She whimpered, but did not move away from my hand.

"Are you lonesome, girl?" I asked her quietly. "Would you like to be free to roam with your own kind? Is that a lover you hear calling you out there?"

Revva licked my hand and wagged her tail, pushing her body up against me.

"Just checking," I said. "But I'm glad to know you'd rather stay with us."

I gave her one final pat and rose to go with Wynn.

Chapter Twelve

Summer

We were already enjoying some early vegetables from our garden. Wynn had been right. Due to the dog team being tethered in the area, we were not bothered by raiding rabbits or rodents. The vegetables were free to grow in the hot, summer sun, unhampered by marauders.

When the summer became unusually hot and dry, even the pesky mosquitoes thinned out some. It was just too dry for them to do much hatching.

About three times a week I went to the garden with my water pail and spent most of the morning watering my plants. It was hard but rewarding work. Between the water that I poured on them, the warmth of the sun, and my words of encouragement, they prospered.

I longed to share my garden as soon as some of the plants were big enough to use. I took a few vegetables to Louis LaMeche, the trader, first. He accepted them with a scowl and no thank you.

I then decided to share some of my carrots with the Indian women. I was sure that once they tasted them they would want more. It was hard to find a woman I could approach close enough even to offer my produce. When they saw me coming they either walked the other way or else went into their cabins.

At last I found a young woman who was unable to avoid me. I handed her the small cluster of freshly pulled carrots, explaining that they added much flavor to the stew. She took them and walked away. I watched in anticipation, but as soon as she thought I would no longer be looking, she threw them in the bush by the path and wiped her hand on her skirt. With a pang, I realized I still had a long way to go to make friends here.

We desperately needed rain. Wynn was beginning to get concerned. The forest was getting too dry. Animals were being driven out into the open areas looking for food. The forest floor was brittle under foot. Our small stream was only about half its usual size.

I didn't know enough about this part of the country to have intelligent concern, but I could see the worried lines crease Wynn's brow as he looked to the west in the hope of spotting rain clouds, and I knew that the lack of rain was a real issue.

I could see the Indian people looking to the skies as well. I even heard them talking in low, frightened voices as I went by. Then I began to notice renewed glances my way and nodding of heads, and I knew that the lack of rain and the pale-faced woman were somehow connected in their thinking. Then I *did* get worried.

One day as I walked the path to the garden I heard the words, "Bad omen," and saw the thrust of the chin my way as I went by. I knew that they were speaking of me.

I wanted to eavesdrop further, but I forced myself to keep on walking. All the time I was in the garden, I prayed. I hardly knew what to say in my prayers. The facts were all so scattered as far as I was concerned, but I prayed on, trusting that my God knew far more about the circumstances than I did.

"Lord," I said, "I really don't understand what is going on here. The people of the village are so steeped in their pagan belief. I don't know how to help them, God, but I don't want to be guilty of driving them even further from You.

"It's all tied up in this garden spot and the fact that we planted here. Now I'm afraid they think the rain is not falling as a punishment to me, and that all of them, and the animals of the forest, will have to suffer because of it.

"I don't want that, Lord. I don't know what to do about it. We do need rain. Wynn is worried about it. Lord, I don't even know what to ask You for, but if you could turn my mistake into something good, I would be so thankful.

"Certainly, the reasonable thing to me would seem to be for You to send rain. That would water the ground, replenish the food supply for the animals and fill our stream again. It should help our problem with the villagers, too. Then they might understand that I really had nothing to do with the drought.

"But I leave it in Your hands, God. Help me to be patient and to do things Your way. I can't untangle this myself. Thank You, Lord, for hearing me. Amen."

I guess I expected to see a "cloud the size of a man's hand" when I lifted my eyes heavenward, but there was none. I scanned the sky in each direction, but it remained brassy bright with sun. I had prayed for patience; I knew I was going to need it in the days ahead.

Then a strange peace came to my soul. I didn't know what or how, but I had the assurance that God had heard my prayer and was going to act on my behalf.

I left the garden and hurried home. I didn't want to get soaked on the way, I guess. When I got to our cabin, I wrestled with the empty rain barrel until I had it properly positioned under the crude downspout on our roof. We hadn't had water in that barrel since early spring. In fact, it had dried out to such an extent that I wasn't sure if it even would hold water. Still, I positioned it, feeling as I did so the many pairs of curious eyes upon me.

"I do hope that Wynn took his slicker with him," I said to Kip who was idly watching my activity. "He could be soaking wet by the time he gets home."

Kip yawned and laid his head on his paws. It was clear he was unimpressed.

"You just wait," I told him. "You'll see."

I might have spoken softly to the dog before me, but in my heart I knew that the words were really directed toward the women who peeked through the overhanging branches, slyly watching to see what the crazy "pale face" was doing now.

Wynn came home several hours later as dry as he had left that morning. It hadn't rained a drop.

"What's with the water barrel?" he asked me, and I felt my face flushing. There was little use trying to be evasive so I decided to tell Wynn exactly what had happened.

"I can't explain it," I said honestly, "but when I was praying this morning, asking God to help break the barrier among the people, I felt strongly that He was going to answer my prayer."

Wynn's eyes held mine. He did not question me.

"Wynn," I went on, "are you aware that they are blaming me and my garden for the fact that it hasn't rained?"

"I've heard little snatches of rumors," said Wynn.

Surprised that he had kept it to himself, I asked, "Why didn't you tell me?"

"What good would that have done? It would only have upset you. There is nothing that can be done about it anyway."

I knew Wynn was right. I could do nothing. I

would only have fretted about it.

"But go on," prompted Wynn. "You were telling me about your answer to prayer."

"Well, I just felt so sure—so at peace, that I . . . I . . . I think that God is going to do something about it. I feel sure that He will send rain."

Wynn smiled and whispered, "Well, praise God." Then he looked back at the rickety barrel. "I'm not sure how much that poor old barrel will hold, no matter how much it rains, Elizabeth."

"I don't really care," I stated, "I just . . . I just . . . well, I wanted to let Him know that I believed Him, that's all."

There were a few moments of silence as Wynn and I looked deeply into one another's eyes. Then he stepped forward and laid a hand on my arm.

"Get some old rags, Elizabeth, and I'll get the tar, and we'll stuff those holes the best we can," said Wynn.

With a grin I went to do his bidding.

We worked together on the barrel. Some of the cracks were quite wide. We weren't really sure if it would hold water even when we were finished with it. All the time we worked, we could sense the villagers watching us.

When we had done our best, we positioned it once more below the spout, making sure that the plank nailed along the roof was slanted correctly to send the water toward the barrel, and then we went in to have our supper.

All night long I expected to hear rain. Even in my sleep, one ear was attuned. No rain fell. In the morning I was sure I would waken to clouded skys, but the sun shone brightly into the one small window.

Kip and I left the village by our usual path. I greeted women and children along the way. They passed me by with downcast eyes and reproachful looks. I prayed inwardly and looked to the sky, hoping to see that one little cloud. The sky was cloudless, the sun already glaring.

"I don't understand, Lord," I whispered.

"Be patient," came back the inward reply.

"Lord, give me the patience!" I cried. "I have never been patient. You know that."

"Then trust Me," said the inner voice. "You have always been able to trust."

"Lord, I trust You. I trust You completely." I knew as I said the words that they came from an honest heart. I did trust Him! I did! I might not understand His workings, but I did trust His ways.

Chapter Thirteen

Panic

All that day I watched for the rain. Nothing happened. There was not a cloud in the arch of blue above us.

That night, I again lay awake for the first part of the night. There was not a hint that a wind was arising to bring in a storm. At last, sheer fatigue called me to sleep.

The next morning, the sun was already up, sending shivery heat waves back from the earth. It promised to be even hotter than the day before. Cracks were showing in the ground where the thirsty soil had long since lost all its moisture.

I took Kip and went to the garden. I talked to God on the way there.

"Lord," I explained. "This pail in my hand does not mean that I don't trust You. I know that You are going to answer my prayer. Bringing rain seems like the logical way for You to do it, Lord—but it might not be. Now, in the meantime, I have my garden that You have blessed with growth. I think You expect me to do my part, so I will continue to water it,

Lord, until You tell me not to."

I tied Kip to a sapling well away from the other dogs, and proceeded to scoop water from the decreasing stream to give a drink to the thirsty plants.

Even with my careful ministrations, it was apparent that the plants were also suffering from the drought. Water as I might, I could not do for them what just one good rain sent down from God's heaven could do.

I saw the drooping plants and I knew they were crying not just for drops of moisture but for a good soaking of the earth.

Carrying the water was back-breaking work. I stood to rest and looked heavenward again. The western sky was clear and bright. The southern sky was a haze so dazzling I could not even look upon it without squinting my eyes.

I turned to the north. Another cloudless sky. And then, by habit, I looked eastward.

There was a strange cloud in the east. My heart gave a little skip. Would our rain come from the east instead of the west or north as usual?

I smiled to myself. Wasn't that just like the Lord, to do something out of the ordinary so that there would be no doubt as to its coming from Him?

I looked closer at the cloud. It was raising up in strange, billowy puffs of brown and gray. It seemed to be originating from the land, not the sky. I couldn't understand it.

I continued my watering until my back was so

sore I could do no more. I soaked and soaked the earth, pouring on bucketful after bucketful. Kip whimpered at me, to let me know that he thought that I was really going to extreme.

"I know," I told him. "It is getting late but they are so thirsty. They seem to just be begging for more. I'll come—soon." And I continued to pour on more water.

By the time I left the garden, much of the eastern sky was under the strange cloud. Kip whined at me and pulled against his leash. He was in a hurry to get home.

There were people everywhere I looked when I entered the village and always they stood studying the eastern sky, pointing and exclaiming excitedly to one another. They shook their heads and chattered nervously, but when they spotted me they hurried away, giving me the path totally to myself.

I was almost to our cabin when I heard children calling to one another. "Fire!" they screamed at one another. "Fire come!"

I looked to the east again and the truth of the words hit me. Fire! Of course it was.

Panic seized me. I had no firsthand knowledge about a forest fire, but if the little I had heard was true, we were all in mortal danger.

I shoved Kip into the cabin and pulled the door shut behind him. Then lifting my skirt, I headed for the trading post on the run.

"Oh, dear God," I prayed, "if only Wynn were

here. He'd know what to do."

But Wynn wasn't in the village. As far as I knew he was many miles to the west. He had left the day before on a trip that would take him three or four days. He had carried plenty of provisions just in case he was held beyond that third or fourth day. I knew that Wynn would not be home in time to tell us what to do.

When I reached the store, the trader was already outside, surrounded by many nervous and chattering villagers. They all seemed to talk at once and he tried to hush them and keep them under control, but I could tell that he was just as concerned as the rest of us.

When he saw me he nodded his head toward the door of his store, and I understood him to mean that he wished to speak to me privately.

As soon as he broke away from the people, he came in. I met him at his counter, my agitation showing in my breathless question, "This is bad trouble?" My nervousness made my limited grasp of the Indian dialect all the more difficult, but I knew even without his answer that he thought it was serious.

"Coming this way?" I asked next.

"It is," was all he said.

"How much time?"

"Hard to say. If wind starts to blow, it could travel fast. If it rain—" He shrugged.

Rain! I latched onto the word. Rain! Of course.

Why hadn't I thought of that? God was using the fire to get everyone's attention before He sent the rain. I smiled and turned to Mr. LaMeche.

"Rain stop fire?"

He looked at me with questioning eyes. I knew he must think me a little mad. He did answer me though. "Good rain—yes. If it come soon."

"Good," I answered, and started to move around him to go out the door.

"Mrs. Delaney," he stopped me, "if rain does not come soon—very soon—then whole village be burned. We cannot stop forest fire. We have nothing to fight with. We can only run—or fry like chickens."

I stopped long enough to let his words sink in, then asked slowly, "Run where?"

"I do not know," he responded and his shoulders sagged.

I wanted to tell him not to worry, to be patient and trust in God, but I didn't know how to say the words in either Indian or French, so I just smiled again and went on out the door.

I looked to the west. Surely the rain clouds would have to be showing by now. There wasn't much time left. But the sky was still clear. The smell of smoke was heavy in the air, and I was smart enough to know that the smell was not coming from the cooking fires.

All around me people were milling about, concern and fright showing in their faces.

There were few men in the village. They had all

left four days before to attend a feast and rain dance at another village two days' ride away. Now we had only those who were ill, or old, or too young to participate in manly affairs. It was not a comforting thought.

I looked at the nervous women. Crying children clung to the skirts of some of them. Older children gathered in groups, pointing at the sky and chattering in alarm.

I knew the fire was much closer by now. I decided to run to the open meadow where I could get a better look.

It was even worse than I had feared. The whole eastern sky seemed to be one boiling smoke cloud. You could hear the crackling of the flames, and the snap as large pine trees split wide open with the intensity of the heat. Bits of debris were carried sunward, and the wind, which had seemed to come from nowhere, carried them forward to plant new fires, leading the way for the giant flames leaping behind them.

I looked once more at the sky. There was no rain.

"Father," I prayed, my voice breaking, "I don't understand this, but I do trust You. What do I do now?"

When I lifted my head I caught sight of two empty wagons Wynn had left beside the small clearing. In the corral nearby, their eyes rolling in fright and their nostrils flaring as they snorted at the unwelcome smell of smoke, tramped the horses that had pulled those wagons. Grasping my skirts in my hand, I ran toward the trading post.

Without waiting for Mr. LaMeche to say anything, I flung an order his way. "Put harness on horses and hook to wagons. I find drivers." I didn't even wait to see if he would follow through with it but turned and ran on.

A group of frightened women stood by the path. "Get ready to go," I called to them. "Gather everything you can and put it on your backs, and then go to lake," I said, gesturing to emphasize my words.

They stared at me. I knew they had understood my Indian words—that was not the reason they were hesitant. It was because of who I was that they questioned me. The thought made me angry. "Go!" I flung at them. "Do what I say!"

In the panic of the moment, they acted on my words and scattered to do my bidding.

I ran toward a group of huddling young boys and picked out the two I considered to be the most likely to be able to handle horses.

"You and you," I said, pulling them forward, "run to corrals and help trader harness horses. When they are hitched to wagons, drive through village and gather up all who cannot walk; then go to lake."

They just looked at me, their eyes large with fear and hesitation.

"Go!" I said, giving them a little push in the right direction. They started hesitantly toward the corral.

"Run! Quickly!" I called to them, and they ran.

I turned to the rest of the boys. "Tell everyone in village to grab what they can and run to lake. Hurry! We do not have time. Everyone! Those who cannot run go in wagons. Run!"

They scattered and I could hear them yelling the warnings and commands as they ran.

Soon the whole village was alive with activity, people hurrying to the lake with hastily gathered packs on their backs. Mothers bundled up children and sent them running ahead; then they picked up younger ones and ran after them.

I watched for only a moment and then turned to hurry to the corrals. Already LaMeche had the teams harnessed and hitched to the two wagons. The two young boys were each given a team to drive.

It was not an easy task, especially for ones so young with no driving experience. The boys looked as frightened as the horses who plunged and jumped, champing on the bits as they tossed their heads at the sound of the coming fire.

"Go quickly through village," I called to one of them above the roar and crackle. "Get everyone who cannot walk."

Mr. LaMeche looked at me. He was trying to hold the heads of the extra team of horses. They wanted to bolt and he was hard put to hold them in check.

I picked up the slack reins and took a firm hold of the team. I had never handled horses before and this was a poor time to be choosing to learn, but I could see no other option.

"Go with him," I called to LaMeche. "Get what you can from trading post, then see if everyone has left."

He did not let go of the horses but stood questioning my command.

"Go!" I screamed. "We not have time."

He went then and the horses reared the moment he let go of their heads. For a moment I feared I would not be able to hold them. They pitched wildly, tearing at the reins in my hands. I brought a rein slapping down across the sorrel's flank, and it seemed to be enough to bring the horses to their senses.

Running behind them, I managed somehow to get them to the spot where our cabin stood. I will never know how I managed, except that God was with me, for somehow I was able to get that pitching team hooked to that wagon. I thought of our few belongings in the cabin and wondered how I would be able to both control the team and collect our few necessities.

I was still wondering when a young Indian woman appeared.

"I hold!" she cried. "You get pots to cook."

"No," I called back. "Don't wait. Drive them to lake. Take wagon right out in water. Do you understand? Drive out far in lake."

She nodded and then, wildly plunging, the team was gone, the woman calling to the horses and urging them on. The wagon was heavy but the horses left the village at a gallop, weaving in and out among the cabins and their surrounding trees.

I did not stand to watch them leave. Kip was still in the cabin. I rushed to the door and threw it wide for him.

"Run!" I screamed at him. "Run to the lake." But Kip stood whining, refusing to leave without me.

I waited only long enough to hurriedly grab around me for anything that my hands touched. As I pulled things off the wall or from the cupboards, I threw them onto the blankets on our bed. Then wrapping it all up together in one large backpack, I heaved it over my shoulder, and Kip and I started for the lake as fast as we could.

The air was heavy now with the smell of smoke. I could hardly breath from the intensity of it.

I came to the stream and stumbled across. My throat was parched and my chest burning with each breath. I was afraid I would not make it. Just behind me I could hear the crackling of the fire.

I turned once to look back. Already the fire had reached the village. I saw the red flames leap up higher as they fed their hunger on the village homes.

"Oh, God!" I cried. "May everyone be at the lake. Please God, may they be at the lake."

And then my cry changed, "Help me to make it, God. Help me to make it."

I cast aside the cumbersome bundle that I was carrying so that I might run faster. All the necessities for our living were in that bundle, but I did not hesitate in mourning. I did not have time. I picked up my skirts, heavy with the wetness of wading through the stream, and ran on.

Someone's hands reached to me from the darkness. A voice coached me on as I ran, and then I felt the merciful coolness of the lake waters. I sank down on my knees, the blackness engulfing me. My last thought was, "Thank You. I made it."

Chapter Fourteen

Reversal

Someone was pouring water over my head. The water was cold. I shivered and fought to right myself. I was in the lake. All around me were people. They should have been milling and wailing, but they were not. There was a deathly silence.

Ahead of me I could see the three wagons. They all stood in water almost up to the wagon box, and at the head of each team someone stood holding the horses' heads. They still snorted and tossed their heads, their frightened eyes reflecting the firelight behind us.

I could see our belongings still under the tarp, piled high on one of the wagons. Another was stacked with articles I could not make out through the smoke and darkness, and the third held silent people. Now and then someone would slip from the wagon to dip under the coolness of the water and then climb slowly back onto the wagon bed again. Nearby, people used cooking pots or pails to dip water and slosh it over themselves or one another.

It wasn't until I wondered about this that I

realized how hot it was. It was a strange sensation. The water was so cold—the air so burning. I dipped my head underwater again and reached up to squeeze some of the water from my tumbling hair.

Behind us was the roar and crackle of the flames. I didn't want to turn and look at the village, but I couldn't help myself. I turned slowly but a hand on my arm stopped me.

"Should not look," said a familiar voice and I realized that Mr. LaMeche, the trader, was beside me.

I could not stop my backward glance.

The flames had claimed the whole village and were moving rapidly toward the stream. It was the only obstacle now between the fire and the lake. Already my face seemed to be blistering from the heat, and the fire was almost a half mile off.

I looked back to LaMeche.

"We be safe?" I asked him.

"Who can know," he replied. "But if we are not, not be safe anywhere."

The lake was our only hope. The water should keep us from severe burns, but would there still be air for us to breathe?

I dipped under again.

"Did we get everyone?" I asked LaMeche.

"I think so," was his reply.

"Thank God!" I cried and the warm tears ran down my face to mix with the cold lake water.

Next to me a child was crying. I moved in the

semidarkness. The mother was exhausted from holding the little one.

"Here," I said, "let me hold him for you."

She gave up the child and I took my hand and thoroughly soaked his hair and face. He squirmed his displeasure but I held him firmly.

"It is coming closer," I heard a frightened little girl say, and I looked up at the flames.

I passed the child to LaMeche and reached out to help an elderly woman. For a moment she lost her footing after dipping into the lake, and she struggled in the chilling waters. She murmured as her balance was restored and I turned back to LaMeche.

"Will the stream stop it?" I asked, but in my heart I already knew the answer.

"No," he answered. "The wind blows too hard, the stream is too dry. The fire will jump like it was not there."

I began to pray again. There still was no rain, though I could not see the sky for the billowing smoke all around us.

I looked for Kip. In my concern for the people, I had forgotten him. He was near me, treading water, only his nose and eyes showing above the surface.

Then I noticed that Kip was not the only animal in the lake. Here and there were other dogs and woodland creatures who had been driven from their homes by the flames. A fox paddled not more than five feet away, and showing just beyond him were the horns of a buck. Rabbits, reluctant to take to the water, ran panicky along the shoreline.

I thought then of Wynn's dog team. They were tethered on the little island! If the stream did not stop the raging flames, they would all be burned alive! I started to weep, and to get control of myself again, I ducked my head back under the water and held it there until I had to gasp for air.

The flames were almost on the banks of the stream when a strange thing happened. I think we all saw it, and yet none of us who watched could really believe our eyes.

One moment the fire was being driven directly toward us, the wind sending sparks and burning bits of charred branches sailing through the air, and then the next, the wind completely changed direction, and the flames were being driven back the other way, turning again to the area that had already been consumed.

We watched in unbelief. Could it possibly be so? Would it change again in another moment? Did we dare to hope? Did we dare?

Even as we watched, the fire lost some of its ferocity. There was nothing more to feed upon. Though the flames still sent up sparks from the burning trees and logs of the village homes, yet it burned more slowly now, and more importantly, the lethal fumes and the stifling air were blown away from us and the wind brought in fresh air for our bursting lungs.

It was then that I heard the barking of dogs.

Wynn's team was still alive! They complained about their lot, but they were still alive.

I breathed another prayer of thankfulness and then looked about me.

"How much longer to stay here?" I asked La-Meche.

"Not safe yet," he answered. "Soon maybe."

I decided to wait for LaMeche to give the order to leave the lake. I had had enough of commanding to last me a lifetime.

It was the animals who left the water first. The things of the forest quietly slipped from the water and bounded off to find themselves new homes.

In the distance the fire still crackled, but the heat was not as intense now. I looked at the villagers in the water. I knew they were as anxious as I was to leave the cold water. My legs cramped and my body numb, I wondered if I would ever be warm again. Except for my face. It felt brittle from the heat. I was sure that my skin was parched and my lips cracked.

The village dogs left the water next. Several of them had been freed by thoughtful people as they fled before the fire. Those who had not would no longer be alive. I shuddered as I thought of them.

The horses began to snort and to plunge again and it was apparent that we needed to get them moved from the lake. LaMeche passed the child back to me.

"I will take out wagons now," he said, and moved

forward, the water coming up past his waist.

As soon as LaMeche started toward the wagons, the people took it as a signal to leave the water. They would be in the way if they stayed where they were.

With one accord we waded toward the shore. The night air felt warm compared to the coldness of the water. I shivered. We had no way of drying ourselves—and we were hungry. No one had eaten for many hours, but we likely did not even have a way to start a fire.

With that ironic thought I looked to where our village had been. *Imagine*, I thought, *in the face of all that and I'm longing for a fire!*

We gathered in soppy, shivering little clumps. Here and there a child cried or a dog on the loose decided to challenge another. The fights that broke out here and there did not even turn heads. We had far more serious things to think about.

In the eery light from the still-burning fire, people began to search out the belongings they had dropped by the lakeshore.

LaMeche came back from tethering the horses. The wagons were left standing on the sands of the lakeshore, the teams tied away from the company of people. They were still skitterish because of the heavy smell of smoke and the crackle of dying flames. They snorted and jumped and kicked, so LaMeche tied them securely in a nearby stand of poplars.

Someone produced some matches and got little fires burning here and there. Around them huddled wet women and children. A few blankets and furs were spread out and children were stripped of their wet clothing and put down to sleep. As many as could be covered huddled under each blanket.

Elderly men and those who were ill were also bedded. The rest of us sat around the fires, still too stunned to even talk.

I had no blanket and I was unable to get near enough to the fire. I was thinking that we needed more fires when a voice spoke to me through the darkness.

"You have no blanket?" LaMeche asked me.

I shook my head. "I dropped it by stream. I had everything wrapped in our blankets but it was very heavy."

LaMeche nodded. "All blanket and furs from post cover old folk," he said, and there was apology in his tone.

I smiled, though I'm afraid it was a wobbly one.

"I am all right," I said. "I am warm now."

LaMeche left me and soon many small fires were dotting the lakeshore. At each of the campfires Indian people huddled for warmth. Gradually they had lost their looks of terror and a few even talked together in quiet voices.

As the night wore on, we took turns, without discussion, adding sticks to the fire. Beyond the stream the forest fire died away. Only here and there flames still flickered and sparks periodically flew heavenward.

The wind slackened and the stars came out. Somewhere an owl hooted. I heard a splash in the lake behind me and guessed that a fish had jumped. Nature seemed to be striving to return to normal again.

I still shivered. My wet clothes did not help. I turned one side and then another to the fire and hoped I could dry out a bit.

Here and there people curled up on the sand beside the fires and attempted to get some sleep. I told myself that I should walk through the camp to see how everyone was faring. If Wynn were present, he would do that. I didn't seem to be able to move. Totally exhausted, I shivered again and wished for morning.

From somewhere LaMeche produced a coffee pot and coffee. I will never be able to find the words to express what it was like to sit before the fire, smelling coffee brew on that horrible night. Somehow it seemed to be a promise that the world would one day be normal again. The trader had also found a couple of battered tin cups. I clutched the cup closely in chilled hands and drank of the dark, hot liquid. I knew that with the help of the coffee I would somehow make it through this nightmare until the morning came again.

Chapter Fifteen

Aftermath

When the dawn began to break, I hated to leave the warmth of the fire. My clothing was still wet and I felt chilled in spite of sitting near the small fire for most of the night. Yet, when the camp began to stir, I knew I, too, would need to get on my feet.

I was stiff and aching in all of my bones. My limp skirt hung about me like some old rag. Underneath it, my inner garments were still wet and chafed uncomfortably at my sensitive skin when I moved. My shoes were squishy and waterlogged. I wished I would have had the presence of mind to remove them the night before. They would have had a better chance of drying sitting by the open fire.

All around me people were stirring. Babies cried, children called to one another, and women moaned in anguished cries as they looked toward what had been their village homes.

As the sun made an appearance we could see the smoke still curling here and there as the fires smoldered in spots. The blackened, desolate area that had been our village was not visible to us because of the trees that still stood between us and the settlement. Perhaps it was a mercy of God that it was hidden from us. I don't think any of us were ready for it.

Now it was a new day—with many challenges facing us. Here were almost two hundred people with no homes, no clothing except what they wore on their backs, and no food to fill their empty stomachs.

I walked back and forth before the small campfire. I hurt so bad I thought I would never feel comfortable again. I worked my arms and legs and rubbed at my back—all the time thinking and praying. I could not have said where my thoughts ended and my prayers began—they seemed to be one and the same.

"Lord," I said, "we need food. I don't know where we are going to get it. But You know. Show me how to care for these people. Give me wisdom—and, Lord, give me help. I can't do it on my own."

I had no sooner come to the end of the sentence when a voice spoke behind me. "Yours, I think so."

I jumped and whirled around. LeMeche stood with my big bundle supported on his back.

"You found it!" I cried with joy.

"Yes. Lucky for you, you drop it on this side of stream. It is safe."

"Yes," I said, reaching to take it from him. "Yes, I remember. I just crossed stream and could not run anymore with it."

A twinkle appeared in his eyes. I had never seen this man show even the hint of a smile before.

"A surprise you could run at all," he joked. "You must bring everything but iron bed."

The pack passed from his hands to mine, and I could hardly lift it.

"Oh, yes," I said, attempting to laugh. "You are right. What do I have here?"

I set my bundle of blankets on the ground and spread it open. I had grabbed the cooking pots. I faintly remembered doing so. I had several items of clothing. I must have stripped all the pegs on the wall, for scattered throughout the clothes I found kitchen items. Cups and plates and cutlery clattered to the ground. I had the dustpan—but no broom. A hammer—but no nails. A frying pan. A coffee pot— but no coffee. Tea—but no teapot. The picture of Wynn and me on our wedding day. A stubby pencil, some writing paper and two of my picture books. No food. No shoes. And three heavy sticks of wood for the fire.

I turned each item over as I looked at it. Why did I select as I did? Or did I select at all? I must have grabbed whatever was closest to me.

I looked at the sticks of wood, wondering how I had managed to pick them up. Then I laughed at myself and threw them on the fire. Perhaps they would make our morning coffee—that is, if I could find some coffee.

"We need food," I said absently. Mr. LaMeche was still standing nearby.

"Yes," he answered me.

I looked up from where I was still sorting through the things I had carried from our home. I would change into dry clothes now if I could find a private place to do so.

"How are the people?" I asked.

"Good. Some lips crack, faces swell from the heat, but good."

"Did . . . everyone . . .?" I hated to ask that question, but I had to know.

"I have each family check. No one not here."

What a relief that was! It was bad enough thinking about the dogs. Wynn's dogs! I had to go to the island and check on the team.

I rose to my feet. There were so many things to be done—so precious little to do it with. I looked about me for Kip. He was playing nearby with some village children. It was hard to believe there could still be play and laughter after what we had just gone through. I shook my head to try to get my thoughts in order.

"I must go," I said to the trader. "I must go to the island and see Wynn's dogs—and garden. Must check my garden."

"Go," he answered. "It safe to go there—but don't cross stream. The fire still burn, though you cannot always see it. It burns deep down, underfoot."

I nodded in understanding and hurried away.

I didn't bother with the steppingstones. I didn't bother with the walking log. My shoes were already wet. I lifted my skirts and waded the shallow stream.

As soon as I approached the island, I could hear the dogs barking. They saw me coming and yipped out their welcome. I looked around me, counting out each one in turn. All seven dogs were present, but three were not barking. Three of them lay on the ground rather than straining on their tethers. I hurried forward.

Flash seemed fine. I ran my hand over his back. Not three feet from him lay pieces of debris from the fire, carried over to the island on the wind.

I went to Peewee. He, too, seemed okay, though he whined as he pressed close to me, his eyes running, as if they had been injured.

Tip was laying on her side, still breathing, though it seemed to be with great difficulty. Her sides heaved with every breath. I didn't know what to do for her. I patted the curly hair and moved on, my eyes streaming with tears.

Keenoo was also down. I knelt beside him and passed a hand over his still form. It was stiff and motionless and I knew that Keenoo was dead.

Franco, too, was unable to stand. I could see his eyes flutter open and then close again. His lip curled back as he sensed my presence. Even near death, Franco would not welcome a stranger's hand. I didn't know if I should go near him, so I left him without a touch.

These three dogs had been staked at the south side of the island, the closest to the ravaging flames. Though the fire itself had not touched them, it seemed as if it had done its evil work.

Morley and Revva both appeared fine.

Though the dogs were tethered so they could all reach the stream when they were thirsty, I knew they must be hungry, yet I had nothing to give them.

"I'll be back," I promised them. "I'll be back with some food."

Wynn had left an Indian boy responsible for feeding his team, but their food supply had been back in the village, and it too was gone now.

I went to my garden. It was limp and parched. The heat of the flames must have nearly cooked it. And yet I was amazed that there seemed to be life in many of the plants. They were able to hold up their heads. Then I remembered the thorough watering of the day before. I had soaked them, and soaked them, even though I had not understood why at the time. But God knew. He had prompted me to water my vegetables.

I looked at them with thanksgiving. They would be more important than ever now. The whole village needed to be fed. Yet, what would one small garden do among so many?

"Trust Me," again came the words.

I turned and went back to the camp beside the

lake, formulating some plans as I walked. Food was our first need, so food would be our first matter of business. When we had been without supplies at Beaver River, Wynn had organized the total village into responsible groups. I would do that now. A hunting party, a fishing party, an herb-gathering party; each member of the village who was old enough to carry a responsibility would be assigned a detail.

LaMeche was at the fire. I was glad to see him, for I was going to need his help.

He had made coffee again and I thanked him as I accepted the cup. My stomach cried for something to go with it.

I set my cup down and dug through the bundle of my belongings, coming up with the pencil and a sheet of paper.

"We need to do things," I stated, and LaMeche nodded his head.

"Do we have any food?"

LaMeche nodded at the one wagon. It was heaped high with miscellaneous items that he had hurriedly pulled from his store.

"What is there?" I asked him.

"Flour, salt, sugar, coffee, tea, cornmeal, baking powder. Most needed things, I think. Not sure. Like you, I just grab quick."

I was thankful that we had at least "grabbed quick." We could have been left with nothing at all.

"We must take it all out of wagon and see it," I said.

"Now?" he questioned.

It seemed like the proper time. At least the people would realize there was some action.

"Yes," I said. "Now. Find boys and put them to work. They can put it all in piles on ground."

We found boys who were more than willing to do our bidding, and I turned back to my list.

"Do we have guns or bullets?" I asked.

"I think I grab bullets. Gun—maybe not."

"Knives to hunt, knives to cook?"

"I check," he agreed.

"Fishhooks or nets to catch fish?"

He nodded his head. It did not mean that he had the items; it just meant that he would see if he could find them.

"We now divide people into groups," I said, "with one person to lead each group. They make fire and shelter. We send someone to hunt and someone to fish. Women go to woods for herbs and roots. Children and older ones carry wood."

LaMeche looked at me, his eyes getting larger with each instruction, his head nodding agreement to everything I said. When I stopped talking he reached for the paper where I had been hurriedly scribbling down our plan. "I will do," he said and took the sheet from me. Then he saw it was written in English and handed it back to me.

"I will help," I assured him.

"You count food supplies," he countered.

That sounded like a good idea. I headed back to my fire and my heaped-up blanket pack and rummaged for another piece of paper. Then I went to the wagon where the boys were unloading and sorting.

LaMeche had been right. We had a good supply of tea, coffee, and cornmeal, a fair supply of flour, salt, sugar, and baking powder. There were several tins of canned food, some crackers, and a few spices.

There were also matches, shells, a few hunting knives, three fishhooks, a length of fishing line, four axes, and some tins of something.

I reached for one of the tins. It was not labeled and the lid did not want to come off, so I gave up. I told the boys they had done good work and then went on to find LaMeche.

He had rounded up several of the younger children to help him tell the people what he wanted. All along the shore, various ones were laying out for inspection the belongings they had managed to rescue from the fire.

LaMeche and I walked down the line, taking stock.

I was relieved to see a number of pots. There were more knives and fishing supplies, and some had even carried their grinding stones with them to the lake. Many of the women had managed to save containers and baskets with food items. It would not last for long, but it would help with a few meals. There were a number of blankets and skins. Though not enough to go around, still they would help to at least protect the children and the older folk from the chilly night air.

We took our census, assigned our areas for family fires, and called for volunteers for the work details.

It was not a problem to get those willing to fish. Several young boys joyfully took the lines and fish-hooks and scampered to the lake. A number of young women volunteered to go into the forest for herbs and greens for the cooking pots.

There were those willing to go to the forest for wild game, but what good were bullets without a gun? Our search had turned up none. We didn't even have a bow and arrow in the whole camp.

"We send some boys to trap—to snare something," I said, gesturing with my hands. It didn't seem possible they would be able to provide meat for so many people in such a way, but there was nothing else we could do.

The whole camp bustled with activity. The empty, despairing faces began to come alive again, and calls and laughter of children rang out along the shoreline. Suddenly we were no longer in the midst of a tragedy but an adventure.

LaMeche and I portioned out basic food for the day for each of the campsites. The women came with their containers for the food staples. Young girls ran laughing to the stream for water, pails in hand, or headed for the woods to bring back plenty of wood for the fires.

Our spirits began to lift somewhat, though we knew the days ahead would be difficult and uncertain.

Chapter Sixteen

Difficulties

We limited ourselves to two meals per day. We were all so hungry that our breakfast, a thin cornmeal gruel and coffee, was gladly welcomed. Each cooking pot fed a small, family-sized group. At my fire I had ten people of various sizes and ages. There was a young widow with two small children, two teenage girls who had been orphaned, a middle-aged widow who was alone, an elderly couple who had no family members to care for them, and La-Meche and I.

Midmorning the boys returned from the lake with four fish. Though they were proud of their achievement, I knew four fish would not go far among all the people. I smiled when I thought of how many the "two fishes" had fed. *Well, the Lord will need to perform another miracle if we all are to eat today*, I thought.

The snaring had produced nothing. The boys who had tried came home discouraged and ashamed. I assured them they would be more successful the next time, but I did wonder knowing that snaring takes great skill, untold patience, and perhaps a good measure of luck.

We kept the fires going and the pots boiling. I divided the fish among the families who had elderly or sick to feed. I pulled vegetables from my garden and put some of them in my pot. At least we would have vegetable stew for our evening meal.

I walked the line of fires, a handful of vegetables ready to hand out where they seemed to be especially needed. I wanted to be sure that everyone had something to eat. For many it was only gruel again.

I was feeling a bit downcast. *If only someone, somewhere had a gun!* I wished. When the men came back they, of course, would have guns, and Wynn would bring a gun with him upon his return. But we needed a gun *now*. It might be three or four days until any of them returned, and with our limited amount of cornmeal and flour, we had to have meat. With so many to feed, the basic foods would last a very short time.

I was so deep in thought I scarcely noticed the barking of the dogs, which was a constant thing anyway. And then I realized this sounded different somehow, and I looked in the direction from which it was coming.

Others in the village must have sensed the difference, too, for I saw women lift their heads, and children stop in their play, and boys hesitate midstride—all looking toward the approaching sound.

And then the most unusual sight met our eyes.

The village dogs had formed a pack and were hunting, Kip leading the chase. Stumbling along in front of them, his eyes wild and his flesh seared by the fire of the day before, limped a bull moose. He bellowed his rage and headed straight for the safety of the lake.

I jumped to my feet, waving my arms in a foolish display of excitement. "Stop him!" I cried. "Stop him!"

Of course there was no way we could stop him. As I watched him lope nearer to the water's edge, I saw the hopes of a meat supply for the next few days disappear with his coming swim.

But just as he neared the water, he stumbled and fell, no longer able to continue. The dogs were fast upon him, and just as fast upon the dogs was LaMeche. He seemed to be everywhere, dragging off animals and pushing them aside, eventually striking a fatal blow to the suffering moose with a blunt club.

Boys ran to help him and claimed their dogs and pulled them aside. With great excitement the people crowded around, exclaiming over the meat that nearly had fallen right into our cooking pots.

The moose was skinned and dressed and portions of meat were handed out to hungry families. I added some chunks of meat to my own cooking pot and sniffed deeply as the fragrance began to waft upward from two dozen fires.

The remainder of the meat was tied and hoisted

high in a tree to protect it for the next day's meal.

I remembered Wynn's sled dogs. I still had not taken them any food except for a small amount of cornmeal mush. I picked up scraps and bones now, and hurried off to feed them while my stew cooked.

We were all fed to satisfaction that night. By now we were dry, our stomachs were full, and we were fairly comfortable. The families had constructed crude shelters of pine boughs and skins. Some of them even had bits of canvas to stretch across small areas.

I had been too busy to prepare a shelter, but I wasn't concerned. I would sleep by the fire again if need be. At least I was dry now, and I had a blanket to keep me warm.

I had just washed my dishes in the lake water and set them out to dry when I heard a strange sound. I looked skyward. It had sounded like distant thunder.

To the west, storm clouds had gathered. The storm was moving our way and looked dark and ominous. I pushed back my wayward hair and studied the sky.

"I know we need rain, Lord," I whispered, "but now doesn't seem like a good time."

I looked around me at the makeshift dwellings. Few of them would keep out water.

I was still standing, wondering what to do, when LaMeche joined me.

"Rain now come," he commented, and I nodded.

"Where you sleep?" he asked, and I broke from my deep thoughts and pointed toward the fire.

"No," he said, shaking his head, "not tonight."

He looked around deep in thought. When his eyes rested on the wagons, he stopped and studied them.

"What is under canvas?" he asked me.

I looked at him with wide eyes and open mouth. I had not even stopped to think about what was under that canvas.

"Supplies," I said. "Blankets, clothes, dishes and pots. Lots of things we need! There are impractical things we cannot use but—"

"Can we take canvas?" he interrupted.

I was surprised that the trader was more interested in the canvas than the contents of the crates.

"Yes," I nodded vigorously. "Take it."

He was gone, rounding up three boys as he went. Soon I saw them throwing ropes off the wagon and freeing the canvas covering it. Two wagons were then lined up side by side about eight or nine feet apart and the canvas was stretched from the one to the other, forming a shelter of sorts. Then with axes in hand, the four headed for the pines.

I turned back to replenish the fire and check on my "family" members. The wind was up now, bringing with it the smell of rain. Thunder rumbled across the heavens and flashes of lightning streaked the sky. I hastened to get everything I could under some kind of cover.

Soon LaMeche was at my side again. With him came sprinkles of rain.

"It is ready," he stated, motioning toward the wagons.

A shelter had been made—the three sides protected by pine branches and the top sealed off by the canvas. It looked wonderful.

"Good!" I exclaimed. "Help me get everyone under."

"It is for you," he argued.

I looked toward the poor, makeshift shelter that held the elderly couple. It would do little for them in a storm. Then I looked at the two sleeping babies, and the two girls and two women who huddled around them, their scant blankets insufficient to cover their frames. "Please," I said to the impatient trader.

With a shrug of his shoulders he followed my bidding.

We got all ten moved just in time. We had no sooner set up under the canvas than the rain began to fall heavier. The rain we had prayed for had come.

There was no room under the canvas for another sleeper, so I wrapped a bearskin rug around me and went back to the fire.

LaMeche was there, smoking his cigarette. I wondered where he had found the "fixing." It was the first time I had seen him smoking since the fire.

He scowled at me and turned back to the sputtering flames. I said nothing but reached for a stick of wood."

"No," he stopped me. "No use. Very soon now it will go out because of rain. No use to waste wood. We need it more later."

I listened to what he said, wanting to protest, but I knew he was right. We could not keep a fire going in the rain. Already there was only a small flame, fighting to stay alive, and then as I watched, it too sputtered and died.

So, I would have to manage without even the small comfort of the open fire. I shivered in my bearskin. My feet were sopping wet again, and my dragging skirt seemed to be soaking up the rainwater like a sponge. Soon I would be completely soaked.

I lifted the skirt out of the puddle and tucked it more tightly around me. LaMeche still stared ahead saying nothing.

I deplored the silence. I disliked the black look. I hated being so cut off from another human being.

I tried for conversation.

"I am glad for all your help today," I said. "I don't know what I do without you."

There was no reply.

Boldly I spoke again, softly, because I didn't know how this man might respond.

"When I get up in morning and look at all people—and I know Sergeant Delaney not here to care for them, I don't know what to do." I waited for a moment and then went on slowly, "I pray . . . I pray a lot. I ask God what to do—but I . . . I ask for something more. I ask Him for help."

I looked directly at the sullen man.

"He answer me," I whispered. "He send you."

I watched his face only long enough to see the muscles twitching in his jaw, and then I dropped my gaze.

We both sat in silence now, the heavy rain falling in sheets around us. I stole another glance toward LaMeche. He no longer had his dark, angry expression. He pulled on his cigarette, sending up little puffs of smoke around him, making him squint his eyes.

I could hardly see his face through the storm, but I noticed little rivers sliding down his cheeks and I wondered if it was all from the rain. I still said nothing.

He brushed a hand across his face.

"You are stubborn woman," he said, but there was no malice in the words.

"I know," I admitted quietly.

"You saved village, you know?"

"Not true, I only—"

He broke in, "No one else think. We all run around in circles, and then it be too late to run."

I did not know what to say, so I remained silent.

"Now you sit in rain while everyone else sleeps."

I looked around me at the crude dwellings. I was sure not too many of our number were really comfortable where they were. Very few, I guessed, were getting much sleep this night.

But perhaps LaMeche thought—"I not ungrateful for what you do for me," I tried to explain. "Shelter very nice—best one. I not think to arrange wagons and—"

"But someone else need it more?"

"Yes. Yes. Old folks and—"

A chuckle stopped me. I looked up in surprise. I could no longer see his face through the rain and darkness, so I could not read there what might be making him laugh so unexpectedly.

"Women!" he said, "They are strange creatures. They want most—but they accept least."

"I beg your pardon?" I asked, not understanding him.

"You. You trim window with fancy curtains, you brush dog like he was toy, you fluff up hair like going to party, and then—this. When there is nothing, you give away little you have to people stronger than you, and you go without."

He laughed again.

I was afraid I was being mocked. Then his words came softly through the rain, "I had forgotten. It was way of my mother also."

"I'm sorry—about your mother," I whispered.

There were a few moments of silence; then he spoke again.

"She Indian," he said. "She not fuss with curtains or hairdos. But she like pretty things. She make beaded vests and moccasins with beautiful designs. She hunt wild flowers just to study them. She point out to us rainbow, sunset." He stopped again. "But she was fighter, too. She last to give up when fever took us. She nursed others when she could only crawl. She gave me last medicine when she need it more." He hesitated again. "She Indian," he said, "but she much like you."

I blinked the tears from my eyes. It was the nicest compliment I had ever been paid, and it brought a big lump to my throat.

"Thank you," I whispered in English, just before the thunder cracked and a fresh outburst of rain came sweeping down upon us.

The night was cold and wet, the fire was out, we sat and shivered in our bearskins that offered us little protection, but somehow a new warmth was stealing through me.

Chapter Seventeen

Counting the Days

Uncomfortable in their soggy beds, people began to rise earlier than usual. A steady rain still fell the next morning. Wet and miserable, they crawled from a cold bed to a cold day. Children cried and women hushed them in quiet tones, as miserable as their offspring. I was glad I hadn't bothered to change my clothing.

A few of the women made attempts to get a fire going. The wet wood smoked and sizzled but produced no flame. There would be no hot gruel, no hot coffee or tea to warm up cold bodies.

I fed my group leftover cold stew from the night before and prayed that the rain would soon cease.

LaMeche asked my permission to use a team and the remaining wagon. I didn't ask what he had in mind but nodded agreement. I was surprised he assumed that I had the authority to respond one way or the other.

He gathered some of the older boys, and they set off toward what had been our village. I wondered briefly about their mission but was too busy serving stew to ask.

In about an hour's time they were back. By their cargo and sooted hands and clothing, it was evident they had been rummaging through the ashes of the village. Three small, blackened cookstoves were on the wagon, plus a number of sooted pots and hand tools. My smoke-darkened washtub and scrubboard also were on board. They also had a small amount of charcoaled lumber that had not burned completely in the fire.

With my hammer and the trader's nails, they began to construct a shelter of sorts. There was not enough lumber to fill in the sides, but at least an overhang was provided. Then skins were thrown over the lumber and two of the stoves were moved under the canopy.

It was not long until a fire was going in each of them. The children were sent to the woods to bring back sticks to feed it, and the women excitedly moved their cooking pots onto the stoves.

We had to take turns in the shelter. It seemed to take most of the day to get one round of meals cared for. Many of the children wanted to huddle around the crude kitchen trying to catch a little of the warmth from the fires, and the cooks had to constantly be chasing them out from underfoot.

What a day of misery! We never did see the sun, and there was no way to dry any of the bedding for the coming night.

Even the beds under the tarp and the two wagons got wet. The ground was so waterlogged that it ran in under the pine branches and soaked the bedding of those inside.

But no one could accuse the storm of being partial—it treated all alike. No one was exempt from the cold and wetness.

Again we sat huddled in our bits of furs or skins or blankets. Like protective hens, mothers tried to crowd all their children under their outstretched arms. The older folk and the sickly were invited to take turns near the cooking stoves. LaMeche took on the task of feeding the fires.

There was no sleep for me that night either. I was too miserable. I stirred around the campsite trying to check on others. It was more comfortable to keep moving than to sit still anyway.

Wynn should be back tomorrow or the next day, I kept promising myself. That was the hope that kept me going. When Wynn arrived, I was sure he would put things to right.

Toward morning the rain began to lessen—not quitting entirely, but it did slow down. I took my turn at the woodstoves to get a hot meal for my "family." I made a big pot of cornmeal, and while it cooked I also cooked my meat and vegetables for the supper stew. I thought it would save time and space to have all my cooking done at one time.

Silver Star, the young widow, came to join me.

"I work now," she said. "You rest."

I thought as I listened to her soft voice that she should have been called Silver Tongue rather than Silver Star. Her voice was soft and musical like a gently flowing brook or a trilling songbird.

"If you watch pot I go feed sled dogs," I said, smiling at her.

She nodded and I turned the stirring stick over to her and left the enclosure.

LaMeche was busy slicing up meat portions for the day's supper meal. I asked him for some of his scraps and started out for the small island.

I was reminded that I had not been back to see the dogs since the day the moose had been killed. I had sent some of the boys across with some food scraps for them and had promised myself I would check on them later. I had forgotten. I chided myself for not taking better care of the team. I should have done something for Tip and Franco. I had been so busy caring for the people that the dogs had slipped my mind. *Well*, I told myself, *I have no idea what I could have done for them anyway.* Still I felt that I had failed Wynn in this. I knew how important a good team was to him.

When I reached the stream, I could not believe my eyes. The steppingstones could not even be seen and the fallen log that stretched from bank to bank was under water as well. *How will I ever get across?* I despaired.

I looked down at my clothes. They were already

wet. My shoes sloshed with every step I took. I decided I couldn't be much worse, so without even hoisting my skirt, I waded into the swiftly flowing little stream.

Unprepared for the strength of the current against the sweep of my heavy clothing, I stumbled, hardly able to keep my balance against it. I finally righted myself and made it to the other shore.

The dogs were glad to see me. I think they wanted companionship just as much as food. They pressed against me, leaving the meat scraps momentarily untouched as they licked my hands and waved their whole bodies.

Someone had removed Keenoo. I had told LaMeche about the dog, and I surmised he had been the one. Another post was vacant also. I saw the leash dangling from the stake where the dog had been tethered. I had to look around the circle and review the dogs in my mind before I knew which one was missing. Tip, too, must have succumbed to the smokey fumes from the fire.

Franco was on his feet, but he looked weak and wobbly. He breathed with a raspy sound, and I wondered how badly his lungs had been damaged. Perhaps he would never be able to pull the sled again.

I fed them all, gave pats where they were welcomed and talked to each dog in turn, and then I pulled some vegetables from my garden and started back to the campsite. I did not want the stream to get any deeper or swifter before I made my way back across, and the rain and runoff were still feeding it.

When I got back to the lakeshore, Silver Star had already served the cornmeal. She and Small Woman, the other widow, were washing up the dishes in the lake. They smiled when I came near.

"You eat now?" invited Small Woman as she handed me the bowl she had just washed.

I smiled my thank you and went to dish up my cornmeal. It was hot. That was about all one could credit it with. Though not tasty, it was filling and, under the circumstances, we were thankful to have it.

Kinook, the older of the teenage girls, brought me a tin cup filled with coffee. She smiled shyly as she handed it to me, and ducked her face to avoid eye contact.

"You bring me joy," I said in her native tongue. There were no words for thank you.

Her face flushed. She turned from me, but not before stealing one little glimpse of my face.

"Kinnea and I find dry sticks," she said, and was gone.

By noon there was a break in the clouds, and in midafternoon the sun came out. Its brightness and warmth soon had the earth and the people steaming. *Perhaps*, I thought with great longing, *perhaps we will sleep tonight*.

We spread our blankets and furs on bushes and branches all around us. Everything that could be spared off our backs was hung out to dry. The pine branches were stripped away from the dwellings to allow the sun total access into the shelters in hopes that the ground would be dry enough to sleep on by nightfall.

The children rallied to assist in the tasks. Boys picked up the crude poles with their lines and hooks and hurried to the lakeshore. Girls scrambled into the woods looking for dry fire material. Young women left their young in the care of older ones and went into the pine forest for dry branches for bedding foundation.

Even the younger children became more cheerful, stopping their fussing and resuming their play. Many of them had been totally stripped of their clothing and were running naked in the summer sun.

The elderly moved or were assisted to places in the sun where they could benefit from the warmth of the rays. They sat steaming in the afternoon brightness as the clothing they wore began to dry out.

The Indian women and children were all walking shoeless, and I decided that it was the smart thing to do. However, I still had on my stockings. They were torn and mud-stained, but there was no privacy for me to remove them. Even as I looked down at them and noted their deplorable condition, I realized that now they were the only pair I had.

I constantly watched the trails for any sign of

Wynn. Oh, how I longed for him! Even though our situation was still grim, I felt that things would all work out someway when Wynn returned.

Even as I watched to the west, I saw many of the Indian women looking to the northeast. Undoubtedly they were longing for the return of their husbands with the same intensity as I waited for mine.

But another day ended and Wynn had not come. With a heavy heart I again prepared the beds under the canvas top.

The Indian wives went about their evening preparations, their eyes just as heavy as mine. They too longed for their mates.

I sat down before our private fireside. The big stoves had done their work well, but with the rain-clouds passing on, we were now able to have our fires again. I was lonely. I was weary. Every bone in my body seemed to ache. I was afraid—afraid that LaMeche and I would not be able to get this group of people through another day. Our meat supply was gone. We had no gun. It seemed unlikely that God would drive another injured buck into our camp. But most of all, I needed sleep. It had been many nights since I had a good rest. I was exhausted.

I was on the verge of frustrated tears when a voice spoke softly beside me. "You sleep now."

It was Silver Star.

"There not room," I answered and was quick to hurry on. "But it's all right. I have dry blankets now. Sleep here by fire."

"No, you must sleep good. You go to wagons. I sit by fire."

"But your babies?"

"They will sleep—all night. They sleep good. You go sleep by them."

I was too weary to argue.

"You take my blanket," I told her and passed it to her. She did not object but took the blanket and wrapped herself in it. Then she sat down beside the fire.

I worried about her as I crawled carefully into the vacated spot under the tarp, careful not to awaken her sleeping children or the other occupants of the enclosed area. I hated to think of her all alone in the stillness of the night. But I was too weary to fight sleep anymore.

Just as I was dozing off I remembered LaMeche. He had no place to sleep either. He, too, would be sitting by the fire. Silver Star would have company. Good company. Perhaps he would make them coffee and they would chat about the day's events together. I was content. I let sleep claim me.

Chapter Eighteen

The Gift

Excited voices and many tramping feet awakened me. For a moment the haze of sleep kept me from focusing on where I was and what was going on around me, and then I remembered the devastating fire. We were all homeless and we were waiting for the men to return.

Like a bolt I was out of bed. *The voices!* They were men's voices. Perhaps Wynn was back. I crawled carefully from my bed and peered out into the dawning new day.

All around me men were meeting with their families, and the reunions turned into excited talk. Wives were weeping and clinging to their husbands, trying to answer questions that seemed to have no answers.

I emerged slowly, made an attempt to smooth down my messy hair and looked about the campsite for a glimpse of Wynn. He was nowhere to be seen. Tears stung my eyes. I turned to crawl back to my warm bed when a male voice called to me.

"White woman!" he shouted. I froze in my tracks.

Slowly and reluctantly I turned to face him, and I'm sure my face was even whiter than normal.

I did not speak. The man before me was the village chief, and one, especially a woman, did not address him. That much I knew about tribal ethics.

He approached me, his face void of expression. I did not know what he intended to do. Perhaps he had decided that it was due to the ill-placed garden that the curse of the forest fire had come upon them.

I stood where I was, as custom demanded—with my eyes lowered.

I did not look up even when I saw the pair of brightly beaded moccasins standing not three feet from me.

Oh, dear God, I prayed silently. *Bring Wynn back quickly. Surely he will respect the white man's law— and the lawman—even if he does blame the lawman's wife.*

The chief reached a long, buckskinned arm toward me. I shuddered. I had seen it done before. To sentence the condemned the chief placed a hand on the head of the accused and pronounced his judgment.

But the hand did not travel to my forehead. Instead, it rested lightly on my shoulder.

"You do good," the strong voice declared loudly enough for the whole tribe to hear. A shiver ran all through me. I scarcely could believe my own ears.

"You do good," he stated again. "You save women and children—our wise old ones and our sick."

I shut my eyes and breathed a prayer of thanks.

The brown hand dropped from my shoulder. I waited but he did not move away.

"What you want?" he asked me.

I was confused. I didn't understand what he meant.

My eyes lifted involuntarily to study his face. "What great chief mean?" I stammered in his native tongue.

"Horses? Furs? I give it you."

And then I understood. The pride of this man would not allow him to be indebted to anyone. In his thinking, my saving the village had incurred a large debt. He must pay that debt or be shamed in the eyes of the people. I stammered for words, trying to find some way to tell him I did not see him as indebted to me.

"Oh, no. No, please," I struggled, but he went on naming amounts of horses or furs, seeming to think that his price still was not satisfactory.

His oldest wife slipped up beside him and spoke to him in a quiet voice. He looked at her, his face becoming grim. He answered her as though questioning what she had said, but she lowered her eyes and determinedly shook her head.

He looked defeated, but he squared his shoulders and called to his youngest wife. She slowly moved to his side. In her arms she held her baby boy, her eyes never leaving his tiny face. She clung to him as if her life depended upon it, but even as I watched she straightened her shoulders and her chin came up. She stood beside the chief with the proud look of her people.

The chief spoke to me again.

"I give you best I have. I give you boy child."

I gasped as I looked from the proud man to the timid wife who held the small child in her arms. He was a beautiful baby. I longed to hold him—to cuddle him. With all my heart I wanted to embrace him. The very thing I wanted more than anything else in the world was being offered! I sent up a quick prayer and stepped back a pace.

"Give him," commanded the chief, and the young woman stepped forward and held the baby out to me.

For a moment I held him close, the tears beginning to slide down my face. His somber black eyes studied me closely and then a chubby hand reached up and brushed carelessly at my cheek. I could feel the silence of the onlookers, all eyes on me. The minutes ticked by as I enjoyed the warmth of the baby in my arms. Then I took a deep breath, willed away my tears and lifted my eyes to the chief.

"White woman has glad heart because of gift. He is beautiful boy child. It give me joy to hold him."

I looked up then, directly into the eyes of the chief. I breathed deeply and took a step forward.

"Now I give chief a gift."

I did not flinch as I faced him. His eyes in his

brown, comely face gave no indication of his emotions.

"I give you boy child."

With the words I passed the baby back to his father.

"The debt is paid," I said simply. "You owe me no more."

Then lowering my eyes with the proper respect, I stepped back as a sign to the chief that he could dismiss me if that was his pleasure.

I heard his guttural exclamation, a sign that the little ceremony was now over and had ended satisfactorily. I turned, my eyes still downcast, and made my way back to the shelter under the wagons.

I was glad I was alone. I buried my head in the blankets and cried until I could cry no more. In my arms there was still the warmth of the baby I had just held. Oh, if the chief only knew what he had just offered me! *Oh, if only Wynn would come!*

And then as quickly as I began my sobbing, I brought it to an end. There was a lot of work to be done. I took myself in hand and crept down to the lake to splash cold water on my face. Then I went in search of LaMeche. With the men now back in camp, I decided it would be wise for a man to be organizing things.

I found him sitting on a rock smoking a cigarette. He pushed the stub into the ground when I joined him and then placed the remaining butt in his shirt pocket.

"You look for me?"

I flushed some. I wasn't sure just how to approach the subject.

"Yes, I . . . I'm not sure—men—now back, I not need to . . . to tell what to do."

He nodded in agreement.

"But we need meat," I went on. LaMeche nodded.

"And they have guns."

"Yes," he said. "I give them shells—tell them to go hunt."

I heaved a sigh and smiled slightly as he nodded. I turned to go but he stopped me with his words.

"You like papoose?"

"Oh, yes," I admitted before I could even stop myself.

"Then why you not keep? Chief would keep his word. Would not take boy back."

Tears stung my eyes again. "It not right. A child belongs with parents. You see his mother? Too big price for anyone to pay—to give up child."

"I see," he said, and I felt he really did. "Then why not ask for horses? Or furs?" he questioned.

"But they don't owe me anything. I do what Wynn do if he be here. Not for pay."

"You think not?"

"Of course!"

"There is nothing you ask in return?"

"No, nothing," I shook my head, and then I stopped and my eyes filled with tears in spite of my effort to stop them. "Only . . . only to be a friend—

one of them. A friend. I . . . I . . ." I could not go on.

"It has been hard for you, this past year?"

My lips were trembling so I didn't trust my voice. I nodded my head, wiping the tears from my face with an unsteady hand.

"You shame us," he said softly. "You give—but not to get. From now on, it will take whole village to hold your friends. You will see."

Chapter Nineteen

Misunderstanding

It was hard to get to sleep that night. All the Indian men were now back in the camp, and it should have been a great relief to me. But for some reason they still seemed to expect me to be in charge.

Around each family fire were a number of additional people to feed.

The men did take the bullets LaMeche provided and went out on a hunting expedition. The result was two small deer, five squirrels, three rabbits, and four grouse for our supper. It hardly stretched to all the cooking pots. I again added some of my vegetables to my stew pot. It improved the taste, added nutrition, and made the meat go further. Many of the Indian families ate the meat with a sort of flat bread cooked over the coals.

The returning villagers made more to feed, more to sleep and less room to move. I knew I did not want to sleep out by the campfire, but there was no room for even one more body in our shelter under the wagon.

Again Silver Star came to my aid. She

approached me quietly as I added a few sticks to the fire. Her soft voice sounded like the rippling of water. "The children sleep. I watch fire—you sleep now."

I argued with her but she insisted. LaMeche, coming to the fire with an armload of freshly chopped wood, overheard our words and joined Silver Star's urging.

"You must sleep," he said. "You work hard."

"But Silver Star work right with me all day," I continued.

"But I sleep better at fire than you," she maintained.

"She is right," said LaMeche, "you need some privacy."

I chuckled inwardly at his words. How strange that sleeping under a canvas with two children, two teenagers, a widow, and an elderly couple could be described as "private."

"I stay here with her," continued LaMeche, and I noticed Silver Star shyly dip her head. I smiled. Silver Star was an attractive young woman, and LaMeche certainly could do with the mellowing that a woman and children would bring to his life.

I stopped protesting and went toward the wagon.

The Indian men were not tired. They talked and laughed and visited in the shadows of the dancing campfires. Much of their conversation reached me where I lay in the darkness, clasping the few blankets close to my fully clothed body. Even in the press of many bodies, it was still cold. I shivered and moved closer to Kinook.

I was so tired I wanted only sleep. I closed my eyes, trying to shut out the sound of the voices. They went on and on, calling to one another across the distance of campfires. Then someone decided that since the families had been spared from the fires, they should celebrate with a dance of thanksgiving, or the spirits might think their kindness had gone unnoticed. A few drums which had been saved from the fire were brought out and the beating began. These were enough to make the very earth pulsate with the vibration as the tempo picked up. I felt as if I were trying to sleep with my head on the throbbing heart of Mother Nature. The very ground seemed to rumble with the beating drums and the dancing feet.

Many of the women and children joined the men. Kinook and Kinnea were the first two to leave our shelter. Silently they crawled out, taking their blankets with them to wrap themselves against the chill of the night.

Small Woman left next, not nearly as quiet in her departure. Though she was small of stature, she was not light of foot. She tripped over the elderly Shinnoo, whose heavy snore was interrupted in mid-release and replaced by an angry growl.

Small Woman did not even stop to apologize. She hastened away in the shadows as Shinnoo rolled back over and was soon snoring again.

My whole being cried for sleep, but the beating drums and thumping feet would not allow it. As the night wore on, instead of tiring, the drummers and dancers seemed to get more frenzied. Shouts and laughter often mingled with the chants, and I lay shivering in my blankets, praying that there was no "fire water" in the camp.

It was almost morning before the dancing ceased. Kinnea and Kinook crept again into their places between the sleepers. Small Woman carelessly pushed aside bodies so she could reclaim her spot under the canvas. Soon her snores were joining those of Shinnoo. They made quite a duet. As her voice rose, his snore fell; then his gained volume, while hers decreased. Up and down, up and down, like I was in a rocking boat.

It was to the rise and fall of the snoring that I finally succumbed to sleep.

When morning came, far too early, I hated to crawl out from beneath my canvas security. The sun was already streaking across the eastern horizon. I thought of all the hungry people around my campfire and forced myself to pull free of the blankets.

Silver Star was already stirring a big, boiling pot of cornmeal at the fire. LaMeche was nowhere to be seen. All around were sleeping bodies. The revelers of the night before had not even crawled off to their crude shelters. Men, women and children lay huddled together on the ground against the cold of the night.

Most of the campfires had been neglected and allowed to burn out. Only a few women stirred cooking pots. I knew those who lay strewn around on the shore would be hungry when they awakened. I skirted around them, careful to avoid disturbing them, and after a walk and a wash in the chilly lake water, I went to my own campfire.

Silver Star smiled shyly at me as she continued to stir the pot.

"Did you get sleep?" I asked her, covering a yawn and wondering if she, too, had been in on the festivities.

She shook her head. "About as much as night owl in bush," she said.

Turning back to her kettle of hot cornmeal, she asked, "You eat now?"

Since we did not have enough dishes to feed everyone at the same time, we took turns. Usually everyone was fed before I took my turn, but now with the others still sleeping and much to be done, I nodded to Silver Star.

"We both eat," I told her, and realized I was hungry. "Where's LaMeche? We should feed him, too."

"He borrowed horse and gun and went out."

He must have realized that we would have very little help from the men who had expended all their energies in the night of revelry. I hoped he would have some luck—we were going to need lots of meat.

As I looked around at the sleeping villagers, a heaviness pressed in upon me. *If only Wynn would come*. It was so hard to be responsible for all of them. I didn't want the task. I had not asked for it, yet it had somehow fallen on my shoulders.

I heaved a heavy sigh and turned back to the fire. Silver Star was holding out a dish of the hot gruel. I was hungry, but my stomach had no appetite for tasteless cornmeal again. I took it with a rather reluctant hand and began to spoon it slowly to my mouth. How long would we have to live like this? *Dear Lord, help us*, I prayed. And then I remembered I hadn't even thanked the Father for my breakfast. I looked at it. Could I be thankful? Yes, of course. We could be in this situation with nothing—nothing at all. I was thankful God had allowed us the time to get a few supplies from the trading post. At least we weren't starving. I bowed my head and prayed again.

The children were the first to come looking for food. Because their parents still slept, Silver Star and I were kept busy trying to fill hungry tummies. We cooked cornmeal, served breakfast, washed dishes, cooked cornmeal, served breakfast, washed dishes—over and over again.

I could hear Wynn's dog team over on the little island protesting that they had not been fed, but I had nothing to feed them. It was after the noon hour and still LaMeche had not returned. Very few of the Indian men had aroused. Those who had stirred looked for something to eat, and when they found nothing, returned to their blankets.

The women, too, were still not up. I began to worry that if they slept all day, they would be ready to dance again all night. I even considered awakening them and assigning them tasks in the hopes they would be tired at nightfall. But I was not quite brave enough to do that.

By the slant of the sun it was around two o'clock when the chief crawled from his blankets. Because none of his three wives were stirring a pot at his own fire, he came to ours. I sensed tenseness from Silver Star. She lowered her eyes and shifted her slender body uneasily.

The chief began the conversation with a grunt. I assumed that that was his way of announcing he was now ready to eat. I shifted nervously as well, but actually I was tired and put out with the whole lot of them.

Why should a few carry the whole load? And why should it be the women? Why couldn't he get his braves off the ground and out on the trail for a buck?

I lowered my eyes as I was expected to do, but did not move forward to get a dish of food for the chief. Since Silver Star considered this "my fire," she did not offer the chief food either.

When neither of us moved forward, the chief took a seat on a log and grunted again.

Still I did not move. I stood quietly, my eyes studying the unkempt toes of my only pair of shoes.

"Hungry now," the chief stated in a rather un-necessarily loud voice.

I raised my eyes just a fraction. "Chief honors our fire," I said and took a deep breath, "but Chief not know he is at wrong fire. Camp is broken up into campfires, and this humble place not where great Chief eats. His cooking pots at fire near tall pine trees, a fitting place for chief to eat."

I stopped and waited to see what would happen. Silver Star had stopped her stirring, and I could almost feel her holding her breath. The chief looked at me with wonder in his eyes, then grunted again and stood up. He was going to leave our fire without a word. I breathed again.

Then he stopped and turned, one finger pointed to the pot of simmering vegetables.

"What in pot?" he asked me.

"Vegetables. Vegetables from my garden on island."

He sniffed. Then stepped closer and sniffed again. He looked directly at me, and this time I did not lower my eyes. I had expressed enough submission to his authority. He was at my fire, he was questioning me, I was the wife of the lawman, not under his rule. I stood straight and kept my eyes level with his.

"You grow there?"

"Yes."

"I am told island did not burn."

"It did not."

The chief studied me more closely, his dark, sharp eyes sending messages I did not understand.

"You make strong medicine," he said.

"It not medicine," I corrected him with a shake of my head. "It is food."

"Make strong medicine," he repeated, "to make food grow on cursed island and to make fire turn and run."

And then he was gone, his stiff, straight back sending out signals even in his departure, that he was the chief of his people.

I turned back to Silver Star. She resumed stirring the cooking pot.

"What chief mean?" I asked her in a low voice.

It was not a mystery to Silver Star. She looked at me shyly and then explained, "Chief Crow Calls Loud says you have great power to make food to grow where evil curse had been. When one makes good to come from evil, then one has more power than evil that was there before."

"But—but—" I stammered. "I have no powers—none."

"Then why plants grow? Why Great One lead you from fire? Why you have wisdom to know what to do?"

"I . . . do not . . . Is this what all village thinks?"

Silver Star just dipped her head again, as though in the presence of one greater than she. I was confused and ashamed. How could these people be so—so superstitious as to believe I was some—

167

some sorceress or something? I was greatly disturbed.

Oh, God, I prayed, *Please send Wynn back soon.*

The chief had roused one of his wives, who had in turn wakened some of his children. She turned to the pots, and the children scattered to find wood for the fire. I watched the proceedings, shivering uneasily over the awesome position they had bestowed upon me. Suddenly a new thought came to me. I squared my shoulders, swallowed a couple of times, brushed at the wrinkles in my dirty skirt and headed for the chief's fire.

Chapter Twenty

Relief

Chief Crow Calls Loud was sitting on a big rock next to his family's firepit, his back to his middle wife who was coaxing a small flame to life. I cleared my throat so he would know I wished an audience with him. When he grunted in return, I dared to lift my eyes and begin to speak.

"Great chief gives honor to welcome me to speak to him." I hesitated, searching for the right words.

"I come to Chief Crow Calls Loud to speak of garden. I know my garden is planted on island where none dared to go because of evil spell. I have no power over such evil. I am woman—white woman—who knows little about Indians' spells, and I am not strong against them. But I know Great God of all heaven and earth—same God who made all things and rules over all people." He stared impassively at me, and I breathed a prayer for wisdom.

"He is One who gives knowledge and power," I continued. "In His name I come to Chief. This mighty people of Chief in need because fire took village. We need much food for many people. We need skilled braves to hunt deer and elk and moose." He was watching me very carefully now. He seemed to be interested in spite of himself. I said, "We need many hands to gather pine boughs to build shelters. If rains come again, people will not be warm and dry. We must build now.

"We need young maidens to gather long marsh grasses to weave baskets, and nets to catch fish. Young men who know ways of fish brothers must drag nets so fish will fill our pots to cook.

"We need children to gather sticks from forest to keep fires under pots.

"We must all work together to care for village," I concluded a bit breathlessly. It had been a longer speech than I had intended to deliver, but the chief was kind enough to give me his total attention. When I was finished he nodded his head. He stood silently for several minutes and then spoke, "What does Golden-Haired Woman want from chief?"

"Someone to tell people what must be done."

"You tell."

"No longer. I tell the people when only women and children, sick and elderly in camp. Now men have returned. Chief is back. Not fitting for woman to still give orders."

He thought about that. Then he nodded again.

"You tell me," he said. "I give orders."

"First you must choose best hunters to find meat for pots to cook," I began, concerned that I would need to go over the whole thing again.

The chief called his oldest son. The young man had not stirred since his wild dancing of the night before. I had thought that nothing would waken him, but as the sharp command rang out from his father, he was on his feet.

"Much to do," the chief told him sternly. Then he began to talk so swiftly in his native tongue that I was able to catch only a few words here and there.

The son listened in rapt attention. I gathered as the chief talked that he had relayed my total message. He slowed down near the end and I could follow the conversation again.

"When all done," he concluded, "ask Golden-Haired One if she need more."

I took a deep breath and stepped back a pace. I hadn't expected to be so successful. Even now the eldest son was awakening other men and giving them assignments. Some seemed groggy and displeased with the assignment, but no one questioned him.

The chief then called to his oldest wife and gave her the job of organizing the women for their tasks.

He called the youngest wife and put her to work rounding up the children for the duties of carrying wood for the fires.

In a few minutes the whole scene had changed. From a people sleeping all over the lakeshore in the sun, everyone was now busy with some assigned task. It was unbelievable.

The chief turned back to me. "More?" he asked.

"No." I stammered. "No—no more now. Chief brings me joy, and I . . . I . . ." How did one say "thank you for your co-operation" in the Indian tongue? I searched my mind quickly but came up with no word. "People will eat and be happy," I finished lamely.

I lowered my gaze for my dismissal and stepped away from his family campfire.

When I returned to my own fire, Silver Star looked at me with wonder. She said nothing but busied herself adding fuel to the fire.

LaMeche, who had returned from his hunt, was eating some vegetable stew, and his eyes looked at me with amusement.

"What you say to get great chief to dance to your drum?" he asked me, smiling.

I ignored his teasing. "I tell him we need hands of everyone if we are to eat," I answered simply.

He grinned.

"You have magic powers," he stated.

I spun around and looked at him, my eyes snapping. But I tried to hold my voice steady.

"I have no magic," I informed him quietly. "Magic not needed when work is done." I repeated, "Not magic—*work*," with great emphasis.

He threw back his head and laughed.

I gave him one cold look that only made him laugh harder.

"I think Chief wise. Better not to get you angry.

You are worse than injured bear." And he laughed again.

I could not be angry for long. His laughter was what I needed to forget the heavy burdens of the last few days.

"You laugh," I told him. "You not laugh when you hear what I give you to do."

LaMeche and Silver Star exchanged glances and he groaned.

"No, no!" he exclaimed. "I have done my duty, is that not so, Silver Star?"

Silver Star avoided meeting his eyes again, but she smiled ever so slightly.

"What have you done?" I asked LaMeche.

"I brought meat for your pot to cook."

"You did?" I was excited now. The teasing could wait. "What did you get?"

"One fat porcupine, two rabbits—and one moose."

"You did not—you tease now."

"No, no. I do not tease. Ask Silver Star. She already has meat in pot."

I bent over it to sniff. He was right.

I smiled at him. "Then you do work. We can eat tonight. And I feed dogs. Sled team asks for food all day."

"Do they ask now?" inquired LaMeche.

I listened. I could not hear the dogs.

LaMeche smiled again. "I feed them," he said. "Who can stand noise of hungry dogs?"

I nodded my thanks to LaMeche, fearful that my voice might catch if I tried to speak.

The sun was just hanging low in the western sky when Chief Crow Calls Loud's middle wife came to see me.

"My husband say he want talk with you."

I was apprehensive. What did this mean? Only men were asked to the chief's council. Reluctantly I followed her to the chief's campfire. He did not stand to welcome me but motioned me toward a seat beside him on furs spread on the ground.

I sat down and waited for him to speak.

"It is done. All you say," he informed me. "Hunters find meat. Two deer, one bear. Women carry pine branches, make warm shelters. Tomorrow nets will be finished to catch fish. Fires burn. People warm and full."

He waited and I knew he wanted me to respond.

"It is good," I said.

He solemnly nodded his head.

Then I went on, "Tomorrow men must hunt again. Women must finish nets and young men must fish. We need more baskets. More mats."

He nodded and without further talk I was dismissed. I was returning to my own campfire when I heard a commotion off to the side. Someone was entering the camp from the west-side trail, hurrying toward us.

And then across the distance I recognized Wynn! With a joyous cry I raced toward him.

"Elizabeth!" he exclaimed as he threw his arms around me. "Oh, thank God you're safe," he cried, pulling me close while I held him and wept on his scarlet tunic.

He brushed back the hair that curled around my face. In the absence of a comb I had run my fingers through it and braided it like the Indian people, but the little curls insisted on coming loose.

"I was so frightened when I came back to the village," he whispered in my hair. "I didn't know what had become of you."

I stifled my sobs and tried to speak. "I'm fine. Now that you're here, I'm fine."

"Oh, my darling," he said and pulled me close again.

We did not talk for many minutes and then Wynn pulled back and studied me carefully.

"Has it been hard for you—being here with all these people who—who mistrust you?"

For a moment I was stunned. In the days since the fire I had not stopped to think about the way my situation had changed. Only a short time ago the village people would not even speak to me. As Wynn said, they considered me an outsider, an impostor— but now? Now the chief called me to council. Now all the village did my bidding. Now they wanted to attribute to me magical powers.

I began to laugh. Wynn must have thought the strain of it all was more than I could bear. He looked at me intently, his eyes anxious.

"I'm fine," I assured him. "Fine, and so glad you are back. I missed you so much. There was no one to take charge."

Wynn looked around at the family firepits, the shelters, the meat hung in the trees, the fishnet that was taking shape, the newly formed baskets.

"It looks very well organized to me," he commented.

"I'll tell you all about it later," I promised. "Right now I just want to hear that you'll never leave me again."

I knew Wynn couldn't promise me that, and he knew that I knew it—still, I was glad he held me close for a moment before we turned to the fire and the cookpot to get his supper. He looked at the size of the stew that was simmering. Then he looked back at me.

"It looks like you are cooking for an army," he said.

"Not an army. Just our 'family.' It's grown a bit since you left, and they will soon all be coming for their supper, so you'd better hurry and eat. We'll need to wash that dish you are using about four times before we get them all fed."

Then I laughed and kissed Wynn on his stubbled cheek.

"You were gone so long, I was worried," I told him. "Thank God you are finally back."

Chapter Twenty-one

Reunion

After the evening meal was served to all our little group and the dishes washed and set out to dry, Wynn and I sat around the fire with LaMeche and visited while Silver Star put her children to bed. I had not been watching her, so I did not notice she went to a pine-bough shelter instead of the makeshift shelter between the wagons.

I knew our crowded quarters would not house Wynn now too, but he and LaMeche were talking so I wasn't able to make plans.

Wynn wanted to know all the circumstances of the fire, and LaMeche explained it all in great detail, using all his Indian vocabulary plus his French heritage of gestures. He made such a heroine out of me that I blushed with embarrassment.

LaMeche told Wynn how I had organized the women and children to care for themselves and one another after the fire, and then when the chief and the men came back, I again had gotten things going.

Wynn's eyes were big with wonder. It was so uncharacteristic of me and such a reversal of my previous contact with the Indians that he could scarcely believe it. Now that I thought about it, I found it hard to believe myself.

"They think she has great 'magic' powers," went on LaMeche.

"Magic?" said Wynn. "Why magic?"

"Because her garden grows in forbidden place—the fire stops when it comes to the spot of her garden and turns and runs. She gets all people out of village, and she keeps them in camp. Even Chief thinks she has magic!"

Wynn looked at me as if to ask me whether that was true. I could only shrug my shoulders, feeling uncomfortable.

"I did nothing to make them think that," I protested quietly in English to him. "I only—oh, Wynn! It's so mixed up and ridiculous. What are we going to do now?"

Wynn smiled. "From outcast to goddess, all in a few days. That's quite a switch, Elizabeth," he responded, also in English.

"I don't think it's funny," I protested. "I wish you wouldn't tease. Don't you see the awkward situation? I don't want to be tied in with their superstitious worship."

Wynn reached for my hand. He could see it troubled me deeply.

"We'll explain," he said confidently. "I'll talk to the chief tomorrow." And then he couldn't resist adding, "—if you'll be so kind as to get me an audience."

I swatted at him, but he managed to avoid my playful blow.

The talk turned serious then. Wynn turned to LaMeche. "How much did you lose?" he asked him in his language.

The eyes of the trader darkened. He shrugged his shoulders and answered carelessly, "Only everything."

"You saved nothing?"

"Only what will be eaten by the people before many days are gone."

"None of your furs?"

"Just a few furs and blankets that people use," LaMeche answered.

I had not stopped to think about the unselfishness of the trader. He had held nothing back from the people. Everything he had left in the world he had placed at their disposal.

"I will see if anything can be done for you," Wynn promised.

"And you?" asked LaMeche.

"Me?" said Wynn.

"You lost much, too."

Wynn shook his head. He reached for my hand. "I lost very little," he said, "now that I know that Elizabeth is safe."

I squeezed his hand tightly.

"I am sorry," Wynn went on, "about all my

medicine. I hope we won't need it before a new supply can get here."

"And how you plan to get more?" asked the trader.

"I will see the chief tomorrow and ask his help in sending a runner out to Athabasca. From there I will send word to Headquarters, and they will do what is necessary."

LaMeche nodded. "How long?" he asked.

"I'm not sure. It depends on weather and availability of material and men."

It was such a relief for me to hear Wynn making the plans and arrangements. I settled back, relaxed, and let his words wash over me. The fire flickered and its warmth spilled over me, making me drowsier and drowsier as I listened to the hum of voices. My head dropped to my knees and I pulled my blanket more closely around me.

"What will you do?" Wynn asked the trader.

"I will build again. It will be hard to make start. I have no money. I might have to return to traplines for a few years, but I will work, and I will build." I could hear the smile in his voice as he continued, "Not magic," he said, "but work."

I was sure Wynn would not understand all the significance of his statement.

"What do the people have left?" Wynn was asking.

"Enough," said LaMeche. "They have survived on less."

Then there was only silence until LaMeche said softly, "You must take her to bed. She has had little sleep for many nights. Last night when she might have slept, the braves danced and drummed all night. She will be sick."

I felt Wynn's hands upon my arms. "Beth," he whispered. "Beth, it's bedtime. Come on, let's get you some sleep."

"We can't go to bed," I mumbled. "No room."

"Plenty room," responded LaMeche. "I move all the Indians out of your shelter today. They have own place now."

I hadn't known that.

Wynn bade LaMeche good night and helped me to my feet. I was hardly aware of being led as we zigzagged our way through the camp and over to the wagon shelter.

I was so tired that I couldn't even undress, even if we had privacy. Wynn bundled me close in the blankets and then removed his boots and lay down beside me.

I remember his arm drawing me close, and my whisper, "Thank God you are home," and then I was gone, relaxing in the comforting arms of Wynn and sleep.

Chapter Twenty-two

Starting Over

No one wakened me the next morning, and I slept much later than I intended. I was embarrassed when I finally did get up and found the camp a bustle of activity. Silver Star and Small Woman had fed all of our family, and the two girls had carried enough wood for the day. Chief Crow Calls Loud had already sent each of the camp workers to his or her assigned task.

When Silver Star informed me that Wynn had gone to see his dog team, I did not even wait to eat some breakfast but hurried over to the small island to join him.

I found him bending over Franco. The dog was quite steady on his feet but he still breathed heavily, like an old man with asthma. Wynn's fingers traveled over the dog's chest and rib cage, seeking out the extent of the damage.

I knelt beside him, my eyes asking questions.

" 'Morning, Elizabeth," he said, his serious face breaking into a smile.

"How bad is it?" I asked.

"Pretty bad. It's a wonder we didn't lose them all when you see how close that fire came."

"I forgot to tell you about Tip and Keenoo," I said softly. I knew how much Wynn's dog team meant to him.

"LaMeche told me."

The other dogs were all clamoring for some attention, so I left Wynn and went to pet them, starting first with Flash and then proceeding around the circle. Wynn soon joined me.

"Will Franco still be able to pull?" I asked him.

"I don't think so," said Wynn, "but we'll give him a few weeks and see what happens."

I led Wynn by the hand to admire my garden. He could hardly believe the plants had survived the heat of the fire. I told him about my extensive watering the day before, and he just smiled and shook his head.

"Have you been back to the village, Elizabeth?" he asked me.

"No. There really hasn't been time—and I didn't think I wanted to see it," I admitted.

Wynn looked down at my shoes. "There's something I would like you to see—but it will make a sooty mess of your shoes."

"They couldn't be much worse," I joked, looking at the mud-smeared, rain-stained boots.

Wynn helped me cross the stream, and we started for the settlement.

We hadn't gone many steps until we were in the

charcoal remains of what had been trees and shrubs. The path to the village was no longer distinguishable. All around us were charred stumps and fallen trees that had not completely burned. It was an awful sight.

"What happened to LaMeche?" Wynn asked me.

The words struck terror to my heart. "Did something happen—"

"No, no." Wynn was quick to explain, "I just mean he's changed. He's different somehow. Remember how you used to dread talking to him because of his sullen—"

"He *is* different. Oh, Wynn, I don't know what we would have done without him. He has been so much help. I guess the fire did it." I was thoughtful for a moment. "I guess the fire changed a lot of things."

"Well, some changes I don't like, but LaMeche— I rather like that change," responded Wynn.

"Me, too," I agreed. "He smiles and even laughs. Why, he even teases—mercilessly." I smiled to myself, remembering how I had gotten angry with his teasing, but maybe it helped me to keep my sanity in the process.

"You know what I think?" I went on. "I don't think he was ever as mean and morose as he tried to appear. I think it was all a cover-up. Look at him. He's given everything he had left to the people, without a murmur. No one could reform that much, that quickly, unless they were already like that underneath."

Wynn laughed. "Maybe you're right," he said. "Maybe LaMeche was just trying to act tough."

We came then to what had been the village. It was a sorry sight. Bits and pieces of logs stood criss-crossed where homes had been. True, they had been crude dwellings, but they had been homes nonetheless. Here and there an iron object raised its head through the debris, defying even the fire.

I wanted to shut my eyes to it all, but I couldn't. I studied it carefully as we walked along, trying to picture in my mind what had been there before. I could see the cabin, could picture which dogs were staked out in front, which women busied themselves around the door, to turn from their work as I passed by. I could picture the children playing in the yard, their eyes big with wonder or fright at the strange white woman.

And now, these same women washed their dishes in the lake beside me, the children ran to me for orders, others cooked over my fire or shared from my stew. How things had changed!

"Look here," commented Wynn and I jerked back to the present. We were standing before what had been our cabin. Part of the framework of one wall remained, looking like it would topple over with the first breath of wind but still supporting a few feet of roofline. The plank that had been nailed to the roof at a slant to form a crude water channel still swept along the length of it, charred and burned but still visible.

Then my eyes traveled to follow Wynn's pointing finger. There in front of us stood my "promise" barrel, overflowing with rainwater. I could not believe my eyes. Here and there the protruding rags showed where we had worked on it. The tar discolored much of the outside, but it was holding water!

Tears sprang to my eyes and I could not speak. I felt Wynn's arm slip around me and draw me close. I looked at him with wet eyes and noticed that his eyes were glistening, too.

"Oh, Wynn," I finally managed, "He kept His promise. Right in the middle of the fire."

"He always keeps His promises, Elizabeth," Wynn reminded me.

Then I looked around at the remains of the village. "But it is so different than the way I expected."

Wynn's arm tightened about me. We both stood in silence.

We turned from the barrel and began to look at the scarred wreckage of our cabin to see if there was anything salvageable.

Wynn pulled out the metal teakettle. "Do you suppose it will still hold water?"

"Let's take it and see," I answered.

The metal frame of our bed was there, but it was twisted beyond further use. There were a few containers and crocks, most of them no longer usable. But a few things looked like they would merit scrubbing up.

After we had finished poking around, we headed

back to camp. I remembered that I hadn't eaten breakfast and was hungry. I also knew there was much work to do in the camp and, like I had told the chief, everyone needed to work together. Even though I was glad to have Wynn back to shoulder the main responsibilities, I still had tasks that I needed to attend to.

"I must get back," I told Wynn. "Poor Silver Star has been doing all my work this morning."

"Speaking of Silver Star," said Wynn with a twinkle in his eyes, "am I imagining things, or do I see her casting little glances in the direction of our trader?"

"I hope so," I enthused. "Wouldn't that be wonderful?"

"If the trader thinks so!"

"I hope he does. Wouldn't it be wonderful for him to have a wife and family? Oh, Wynn, I hope it works out!"

"Have you turned Cupid?" Wynn asked me with a sly grin.

"No, I have not," I retorted. "Honestly, I have had nothing to do with it. But," I admitted more slowly, "if I thought I could influence it, I might try."

Wynn laughed and helped me over the fallen log across the stream.

We walked on in comfortable silence. As we neared the camp, Wynn said, "I'm to have a chat with the chief this morning. I had to have some time first to review the damage and formulate our needs.

I expect to send a runner out as quickly as I can get organized. Will you have time to make out a list of things you'll be needing?"

"I'll take time."

Wynn still looked pensive. "I still haven't figured out just how to do this," he admitted. "Nobody can just remember the whole list—and it will hardly do to try to scratch it on birch bark."

"What do you mean?" I asked.

"I don't have anything for writing a letter or making a list," said Wynn.

I smiled slowly. "You know," I said, "there is just no way that my head would have worked well enough to think ahead to grabbing pencil and paper—yet that is exactly what I did."

"You what?"

"I have a stub of a pencil and sheets of paper. When I ran into our cabin, I just grabbed at random, not even thinking—I even got some sticks of firewood," I laughed. "I thought it strange when I saw the pencil and paper, but I guess there was a good reason for it after all."

"I guess there was," said Wynn, giving me another hug.

After talking for several hours with Chief Crow Calls Loud, Wynn spent the rest of the day organizing the needs of the village and making out his list on the paper I had saved from the fire. It wasn't very official looking but it sufficed. When he had finished his task, every sheet of the paper had been covered with the essential supply list.

Early the next morning three braves and La-Meche left on the best horses for the settlement of Athabasca Landing. Wynn had given them instructions as to whom to see when they got there. The braves seemed excited about this new venture but tried not to let it show. LaMeche did not appear to enjoy the thought of returning to "civilization," but he went without question. I saw Silver Star looking shyly from downcast eyes for one last glimpse of him before they had disappeared from our sight. We had many days to wait before the men and the needed materials could possibly get to our campsite.

Chapter Twenty-three

Adjustments

Wynn now had great cooperation from the chief on running the affairs of the camp. Though the chief had not been openly hostile in the past, he had been at times withdrawn and rather arrogant. It was much easier to work together with him in his present frame of mind.

The women chatted and laughed as they did their laundry in the lake water or carried their water supply from the swiftly flowing stream. Now that their men were back, the experience of "camping out" was not a difficult one for them—except on the days and nights when it rained. Even with reinforcements to the pine shelters, there was no way to keep all the water out, so people walked around drippy, wet, cold, and rather miserable. I feared an epidemic of colds or fever, but they seemed to stay healthy.

Wynn found more canvas in our supply wagon that he draped around our shelter. We *almost* had privacy, a great relief to me. I was able to change my filthy clothes and take a bath of sorts. I did as the

Indian women and washed my hair in the lake water. It was cold, and I had no soap of any kind, so it was not a very satisfactory job. But it did wash some of the woodsmoke smell from my hair.

The Indian women now shyly included me in their chatter, even coming to my campfire for a cup of tea.

The children, too, smiled and even waved occasionally when they went by the campsite on their way to gather wood. It helped, I am sure, to have the two orphans, Kinook and Kinnea, at our campfire.

I wondered about the two young girls. I had been told that they had lived alone since the death of their mother, having lost their father several years previously. Now that their cabin was gone, would the settlement people rebuild it for them? Would they be forced to find refuge with another crowded family? Or would they be married off early—too early, in my opinion—to one or another of the village men as a second or third wife?

I wished to keep them with Wynn and me. But remembering our small, one-room cabin and expecting our new home to closely resemble it, I realized there was no way we could crowd them in. I hadn't yet had opportunity to speak to Wynn about them, but I promised myself that at my first chance, I would do so.

Some of the women found a berry patch to the northwest of us where the fire had not burned, and we all set off one morning with newly woven baskets.

Our spirits were high on this bright, clear, late-summer day in spite of our meager existence. The chatter of the women and the giggling of the young girls swirled around me as I walked slowly, enjoying the outing.

Silver Star dropped back to walk beside me. She had left her two young children in the care of the elderly woman who shared our campfire.

We walked in silence for some time and then she spoke, softly, "Has sergeant heard from the braves?"

"No," I replied, "not yet."

Her eyes looked sad.

"Is Silver Star worried?" I asked gently.

She only nodded her head slightly, lowering her eyes. But not before I could see the concern in them.

"You worry about one of the braves?" I asked her.

She shook her head.

"Then you worry about the trader?"

Her eyelashes fluttered and her face flushed slightly. She said nothing.

"He will be fine," I assured her. "He has lived in outside world before. He knows all about it."

"Silver Star knows that," she whispered.

"Then why do you fear?" I asked her.

Suddenly I knew the answer. She was afraid LaMeche might not come back—that he might decide to stay in the outside world where the way of life was so much easier than facing forest fires, disease, and famine far from any help.

"He will come," I comforted, hoping with all my heart that I spoke the truth.

Silver Star dared to look at me, her face still anxious, yet hope shining in her eyes.

We reached the berry patch and all set to work filling our containers. The berries were small and scarce because of our lack of summer rains, yet they tasted delicious and were a real treat after our days on a limited diet. I sneaked a few every now and then as I picked. The others did, too—I could tell by the blue stains on tongues and teeth.

There would be no way to make a pie or can what was left over, but we would enjoy them fresh and perhaps even have a few left to dry in the sun.

We cleaned the patch before we left it, though we had not even filled our containers. We would need to do more scouting in the area to look for additional patches if we wanted further picking.

We silently started for home, walking single file or two-by-two. Again Silver Star walked at my side, but she offered no conversation as we walked and, respecting her silence, I did not talk either.

Nanawana, the youngest wife of the chief, walked just ahead of us, her sleeping son strapped to her back. I couldn't help but watch the child as she walked.

What a darling baby! my heart cried. His black hair and eyes, his pudgy, dimpled cheeks, his tightly clenched fist near his mouth just in case he needed something to suck on reminded me of Samuel.

A tear came unbidden, and Silver Star saw me wipe it away. She looked at the baby, his little head nodding with each step of his mother, and I knew she understood my empty arms.

I was glad when we reached the village and I again was too busy to think about anything other than the tasks at hand.

The days did not change much. Our biggest task was to keep everyone fed. My little garden was nearly depleted. There would be nothing to store for our winter use.

Without admitting it to one another, we soon began to watch the southeastern horizon for a glimpse of the returning men. If we were to have decent homes constructed before the winter set in, we must begin immediately. Every day counted.

Wynn said nothing to me of his concern, but I saw his eyes shift often to the southeast. I knew he was willing the return of those he had sent out.

About sunset of the twelfth day, we had just finished washing the dishes for the last time after our evening meal. A shout went up from someone in the camp.

All eyes quickly lifted toward the southeast where three horses appeared, the riders answering with upraised hands. *Three*—but there should have been four! I quickly stole a glance at Silver Star. Her head was lowered, concealing her face. I knew she was quite aware that one of the men was missing.

How could he? I accused LaMeche silently, knowing that Silver Star's heart would be broken. *How could he do this to her?*

But when the three reached the village and were greeted by the villagers circling around them, it was not LaMeche who was missing. He pushed his way through the crowd and approached our campfire.

I smiled my welcome, more relieved than I dared show, and looked around for Silver Star. She was not there. Sometime during the commotion, she had slipped quietly away.

I saw LaMeche glancing around as well, and I guessed that he, too, was looking for her, though he did not ask. Instead, he picked up a cup and asked for some coffee.

"There is still hot soup, too," I informed him. He welcomed a bowl and sat down at the fire.

"How was your trip?" I asked.

"Good to be home," was his answer.

I knew his report would be given in full to Wynn, so I did not ask further questions.

"It is good to have you home," I said instead.

He sipped slowly from the steaming cup. "Things have gone well?" he asked.

"Yes," I said with some hesitation, thinking of the days of rain and the difficulties of wet clothes and blankets. "As well as one could hope."

Wynn joined us then, and LaMeche stood to his feet, extending a hand. Then he reached into his pocket and produced a bulky envelope. Wynn accepted it, sat down on a log, and slit open the envelope to review the contents. He was silent as he read. When he folded the official letter and returned it to the envelope, I could stand it no longer.

"Well?" I questioned.

"The supplies will be coming just as soon as they can get them through," he said with some relief. "They will also send in some men to help with the rebuilding."

I heaved a big sigh. It was such a weight off our shoulders to know that there would be help coming to furnish the villagers with adequate shelters before the coming of winter.

"How was your trip?" Wynn asked LaMeche.

LaMeche just hunched his shoulders.

I thought he was going to refuse to talk about it, but he surprised me. When he had finished his soup, refilled his coffee cup, rolled himself a cigarette, and settled back on his log with his back to a tree, he began to tell all about his trip out, the braves he traveled with, the people he met, where they stayed, the reaction of the three young men to the things they saw. Then he told of the "fire water" that the three braves had somehow obtained, how they managed to drink themselves into a stupor that eventually ended up in a fight resulting in one of the braves being locked behind bars for a two-month period.

Try as he might to reason and barter, LaMeche

was not able to get the young man released from jail. At last he gave up and was forced to return home without him.

I knew the young man by appearance only, but he was cocky and swaggering even around the camp. It was not hard for me to picture him getting himself into trouble when he reached a place where he was not closely supervised.

"Why did the chief send him?" I asked Wynn later when we were alone. Wynn shook his head.

"Perhaps he thought he needed a lesson—I don't know."

"Have you talked to the chief?" I asked.

"LaMeche went to report to him. If the chief wants me, he will send for me."

Wynn was right. In a few minutes the chief's son came asking Wynn's presence at his fire.

I stirred up the coals and added a few more sticks to our own fire, still wondering about Silver Star.

I did not wonder for long. She was soon back, her eyes heavy. I was about to break the news about LaMeche's return, but she spoke first.

"Silver Star might need to leave your campfire," she said solemnly.

"What do you mean?" I asked quickly.

"Grey Wolf leaves me gifts."

My head jerked up. Leaving gifts was the way that an Indian man proposed to a desired maiden.

But Grey Wolf? He was loud and cantankerous.

He already had one wife and was known to beat her with a good deal of regularity. I held my breath, not knowing what to say.

It was clear from Silver Star's face that she did not like the idea. And then I realized that Silver Star *did* care about the trader and had been hoping LaMeche might make his move before Grey Wolf would demand his answer.

"But—but—" I stammered, "can't you wait?"

"He says he has waited long enough. He looks at me with anger in his eyes."

"Can't you just say no?"

Silver Star lifted herself from her squatting position, her eyes met mine and she spoke softly, yet forcefully. "I am widow, with two small children. I am burden to village people. If someone wish to marry me and care for my needs, it is my duty to accept."

"But—but *Grey Wolf?*" I said, hating the thought. Silver Star lowered her eyes again and squatted down by the fire. Her head and slim shoulders drooped in resignation. She made a pitiful picture. I was reaching to place a hand on her shoulder when a voice behind us spoke forcefully, cutting the stillness of the dark night.

"Never," he spat out, and a curse followed. "Never would I let him take you."

It was LaMeche. He had returned in time to hear at least a part of our conversation. Silver Star gave a startled gasp and involuntarily her hand went out toward LaMeche, but she quickly recovered her poise and dropped her gaze and let her hand fall.

Silence fell and seemed to linger. No one was doing or saying anything. Why didn't LaMeche continue? He just stood there, looking angry and upset, his eyes still on the trembling Silver Star.

I took a breath and moved back a step. I wanted to shake them both. I wanted to make them talk to each other.

"And how can she stop him?" I dared ask rather pointedly.

LaMeche did not look at me. His eyes were still full of Silver Star. They softened, and she glanced up at him, with love and hope in her gem-black eyes.

"By her accept *my* gifts," he said gently, and Silver Star lowered her flashing eyes again. Then she was gone, slipping away quietly into the darkness of the night.

I looked at LaMeche. He nodded at me, his face still serious, and then he, too, was swallowed up by the darkness of the night.

When I reached our fire the next morning Silver Star was already there, stirring the boiling pot with flushed cheeks. I wasn't sure if the new flush was due to the heat or to whatever was causing the sparkle in her eyes.

She was wearing a new skirt as well—one with bright colors that circled the fullness, standing out among all of the worn, faded skirts worn by the rest of us. She had a silver chain with turquoise stones about her neck, glistening in the morning sun.

I asked no questions, though I suppose that keeping silent right then was one of the hardest things I had ever done in all my life. It was obvious that someone had "gifted" Silver Star and that she had indeed accepted what he had given. I was nearly sure I knew the giver.

I did not wait long for confirmation. LaMeche and Wynn soon came for the morning meal. I saw Wynn's questioning eyes fall on the attractive young widow, and then I quickly switched my glance to LaMeche. He attempted to be very casual as he took his place, but I saw him look at Silver Star and his face relaxed. He smiled slightly, and then their eyes met and a promise passed between them. I knew our settlement would soon be celebrating a wedding.

As I passed by Silver Star to get the steaming pot from the open-fire spit, I reached out to give her hand a little squeeze. She understood my message and returned the pressure slightly. I had wet eyes as I served the men their morning coffee.

Chapter Twenty-four

Change

"Elizabeth, do you have a few minutes?"

Wynn's voice made me turn from spreading the few newly washed clothes on the low-hanging bushes. I looked at him, nodded my head, and smiled.

"What is it?" I asked.

"I thought we might take a walk away from the camp and talk for a few minutes," he invited.

I was puzzled. Wynn usually did not ask me to forsake my morning tasks, just to talk.

"Certainly," I responded, sensing that something would be different about this talk. I felt a little knot of apprehension within me, but I tried not to let it show.

We were joined by Kip who spotted us heading down the path that led around the lake. I put a hand out to stroke his heavy coat. He had not been washed or brushed for several days, and he was dirty and matted like most of the village dogs. He was in good spirits, though. Life in the rough seemed to agree with him.

I decided I would not question Wynn until he was ready to speak. Instead, I chatted about Silver Star and LaMeche, sharing with Wynn that they would be married just as soon as LeMeche could build a permanent shelter.

Wynn smiled, knowing how pleased I was about the coming wedding.

We walked to a small knoll overlooking the lake, and Wynn indicated that we should sit down on the grass-covered bank. I lowered myself to the ground and hoped he would not make me wait much longer.

"Is something wrong?" I asked, unable to stand it a minute more when Wynn appeared to be settling himself in for a few moments of silence.

"No. Nothing is wrong," he said quickly, turning to me. "I'm sorry if I alarmed you."

I breathed more easily.

"I just wanted to discuss with you the letter I got from headquarters. I haven't had opportunity, with all that keeps you busy." He reached over and took my hand. "Don't you think that you could slow down a bit now?" he asked me.

"I'm fine," I assured him. "I like being busy. It makes the days go faster."

Wynn smiled but was silent again.

"But what about your letter?" I quizzed him.

"They have new orders for us."

"New? What do you mean?" I asked, my face lifting quickly to study Wynn's eyes.

"They don't want us to stay here for the winter."

"I don't understand—"

"They feel they will not be able to get a proper building up for us in time for winter."

"But you said they were coming soon to build," I reminded him.

"Yes, they are. But the native people must be provided for first. They have no other place to go."

It was becoming more and more confusing to me. I shook my head to clear the fog. Wynn's grip on my hand tightened.

"Let me start at the beginning," he said.

I nodded my head in assent and he began.

"The Force has promised to not only send in the required materials, but also to send in some government-paid men to build new cabins for the people of the village. They also will send in a man to take my place for the winter months. He will be single and will be quite able to spend the entire winter in tight quarters."

I couldn't help but smile, remembering the cabin where Wynn and I had spent the past winter. *How could one have "tighter quarters" than that?* I wondered. But Wynn was continuing.

"He will carry on the law enforcement necessary while the village is being rebuilt.

"They have also taken my suggestion of compensating LaMeche to some measure," he explained. "The trading post will be the first building to be constructed because of its importance to everyone. They plan to partition off a very small room in the trading post for the officer to use as a sleeping quarter. This later will be turned back over to the trader, or used as a temporary lock-up room if LaMeche and the Force reach an agreement. Just like we had at Beaver River."

I remembered the little room in the McLean's store. It had been the place where Crazy Mary had been kept until her untimely death.

"When everyone else has been properly sheltered, they will turn their attention to building a new cabin for the Mountie."

"Then we can come back?" I quickly cut in. I suddenly realized how much I wanted to stay now that things had changed with the villagers.

"They didn't state that for sure," Wynn said honestly. "They did say that it would be considered."

That didn't sound too promising as far as I was concerned. I chafed under such hedging, but I said nothing to Wynn. There was little that he could do about it.

"When do we go?" I asked, with little enthusiasm.

"We are to go back with the wagons that bring in the supplies."

That would not be long then. We expected the wagons and supplies in any day now.

"And where are we to go?" I asked. Then with sudden hopefulness, I continued, "Can we go back to Beaver River?"

Wynn smiled but shook his head. "I'm sorry, but

no Beaver River. It would have been nice, though, wouldn't it?"

"Oh, yes," I said, sighing.

"We are to go to Athabasca Landing."

"To do what?"

"I will work in the office there, supervising the two younger men who will be on patrol in the area. You will . . . I guess you can just be a . . . lady of leisure."

"I don't think I will like that," I said soberly.

"Who knows," said Wynn, in an effort to cheer me, "maybe you will learn to like it."

I stubbornly shook my head. I could not see myself enjoying having nothing to do but make the beds and cook the meals. It would be as bad as the last winter when I had nothing to do and nowhere to go. I had hated it. It had been all that I could do to keep my outlook cheerful so that I wouldn't be a drag on Wynn.

"It will be quite different there than it is here at the village," Wynn went on, knowing where my thoughts were leading me. "It is already a fair-sized settlement. You will find many new neighbors—both white and Indian. It will give you a nice break from roughing it."

I still wasn't sure I was going to like the new arrangement, but I knew Wynn needed my support. When I thought about it, I wasn't sure if Wynn would welcome the new life either. He wasn't particularly fond of paper work, yet he would be stuck with it for the winter while younger men did the patrolling and contacted the Indians. I tried to look a bit more enthusiastic and turned to Wynn with a slow smile.

"Guess we can stand it for a few months," I said, and he pulled me close.

Kip came bounding up to us and nearly pushed me over with his exuberance. I laughed and fought my way upright again, shoving Kip away and playfully rubbing his ear.

"Take it easy," I told him, "we won't go without you—" then I looked quickly at Wynn, my concern in my voice, "will we?"

"We'll take Kip," Wynn assured me.

"What about the rest of the team?" I asked him, hoping that Wynn would not be asked to give up his well-trained dog team.

"I plan to take them."

"You are still short two or three dogs, aren't you?" I reminded him.

"That's one of my reasons for taking them. I hope that soon I will have a batch of Revva's pups old enough to start training."

I was excited about seeing Revva's litter when it first arrived. I wanted to help train them right from puppyhood onward. I knew that was the way Wynn preferred to train his dogs. Living in Athabasca, I was sure I would have lots of spare time to help him.

I stood to my feet and looked out over the little lake. In the distance I could hear the calls of the children in the camp. A loon cried—a lonely, wilderness-sounding cry. I knew I would miss it.

"What did LaMeche say?" I asked Wynn.

Wynn stood beside me, his arm around my waist. "About what?" he asked me.

"About all this?"

"I haven't talked to him—and I don't expect that they told him anything about it when they gave him the letter with the new orders."

"Then he doesn't know?"

"I wanted to talk to you before I talked to anyone else," Wynn informed me.

I smiled at him. "Thank you," I said softly. "I'm glad I was first."

He took my hand then and we started back to the campsite. I knew I would see it differently in the days that lay ahead. Each time I looked around me, I would be thinking, "I will leave this soon." It would make a difference. Undoubtedly the tears would fall at times.

"Wynn," I said as we walked, "there is something that I have wished to speak to you about. I am concerned about Kinnea and Kinook. What will happen to them? Will they be given a cabin of their own again? What if they aren't? I'm really concerned about them, Wynn."

"I am, too," returned Wynn. "I hear that Chief Crow Calls Loud has been looking at Kinook."

I stopped in my tracks and stared at Wynn. "No!" I said. "Surely not?"

"She could be in worse circumstances," Wynn assured me.

"But the fourth wife? Who would ever want such a position? She would be the servant of all the rest of them."

"Until she bore her first child, maybe."

"A child? She is still a child herself. Wynn, that's unthinkable! Can't you do something?"

"Our laws do not govern their marriages, Elizabeth. You know that."

"Can't we take her with us," I blurted out. "Both of them. Can't we get some kind of custody and—"

"Do you think they'd be happy?" Wynn asked softly.

I started to say that of course they would, but even before the words formed I knew it was wrong. The two girls would be happy only in their own village, with their own people.

It seemed a hopeless situation. I swallowed the lump in my throat and took Wynn's hand again. In my heart I prayed for wisdom and God's help as I walked. Surely there was something that could be done—some way to make arrangements for them. I prayed that the Lord would work on their behalf.

The next evening Wynn invited me to go with him to care for the dog team. I went readily enough, but inwardly I suspected that he might have other reasons for asking for my company.

I was right. As soon as we passed from earshot

of the village people, Wynn took my hand and slowed my stride. We never felt free to talk for very long in front of the Indians when we wanted a private conversation. We both knew they could not understand our English, yet we couldn't bring ourselves to discuss a private matter in front of them.

"I had a long talk with LaMeche," Wynn informed me.

I turned to Wynn in my eagerness, forgetting to take a forward step, nearly tripping over my own feet.

"Why don't we sit down for a minute?" Wynn asked me, nodding toward a shaded spot near the path.

We took our seat and Wynn idly picked a blade of tall grass, broke a piece of it and put it in his mouth. I could almost taste it, cool and sweet.

"LaMeche was excited to hear that he will get help in rebuilding and restocking his post," said Wynn. "He can hardly wait for the supplies to get here—but I've this strange notion that it might have more to do with Silver Star than with the trading post." Wynn smiled.

"He is quite willing to share a small room with the Mountie who comes to relieve us." Wynn continued. "Later he will let the Force have the room for a temporary cell as they had hoped.

"After the two of us had discussed this for a while," said Wynn, taking both my hands in his, "he started asking me some questions about you—about how a white woman in these circumstances could have the inner strength and the wisdom to save the whole village from certain destruction."

I was watching Wynn's face carefully, my mind racing ahead to what he might be telling me.

"I explained to him that without God's inspiration and help, you probably would not have been able to do what you did. He looked so interested and so—so *wistful* at the same time that I went on to explain to him about our faith in Jesus Christ.

" 'I wish I had a faith like that,' was his comment. I could hardly believe my ears—" Wynn's voice was full of deep emotion as he talked. "The people here have never showed the slightest bit of interest in Jesus or in our faith when I've talked about it in the past. I told LaMeche that he *could* have a faith like that. I told him that Jesus had died for him—that he could repent of his sin, receive the Lord Jesus as his Savior, and be born into God's family."

I'm sure my eyes were as full of wonder and joy as Wynn's when he said, "And you know what, Elizabeth? LaMeche did just that! We prayed together on a log out there in the woods, and he is now a Christian!"

The tears rolled down my cheeks as I thanked the Lord for this one small light in the spiritual darkness of Smoke Lake. "Oh, Lord," I prayed, "help him to be strong and to grow and to convince others here to follow his example."

"LaMeche said something else that I think will make you very happy," Wynn went on, and then hesitated, driving me mad with curiosity.

"Silver Star had already spoken to him. It seems that she has gotten quite attached to the two orphan girls."

I held my breath.

"Silver Star has asked LaMeche if he would mind if they took them. Kinook will soon be of marriageable age, but Kinnea would have two or more years to be on her own yet. It seems that Silver Star has been as worried about them as you have."

I bowed my head in another prayer of thanks. Then I asked God to also bless Silver Star for her love and concern. I would have no apprehension about leaving the two young girls in the care of Silver Star and her new husband.

"Oh, Wynn," I said, "that's a real answer to prayer. I never even thought of Silver Star taking them. That'll be perfect! They already love her and her little ones."

"But there is something else, too," Wynn went on, "and I think that it will make you equally as happy."

"What?" I prompted, wondering what in the world could make me as happy as that last bit of news.

"I dared to have a talk with the chief."

"And?"

"And he heard me out—very patiently. I told him

of my concern. And I dared to tell him of the concern of the white woman—you. And he nodded solemnly and then passed a decree that no man in the village shall take gifts to Kinook until the frost comes a year from now."

"Oh, Wynn," I cried, "did he really? Did he really say that?"

"He did. And he made sure that every male in the village knows about it, too."

A new, more sobering thought struck me. *Did the chief pass his law to save the young girl for himself?* I didn't like to think of it.

"Why?" I asked Wynn. "Why do you think he did that? Was it to protect her for himself? She is very pretty, Wynn."

"If he wanted her for himself," said Wynn, "there would be nothing stopping him from taking her right now."

"I know, but maybe even he realizes she is still too young."

"Then give him a little credit—even if he does want her for his fourth wife, at least he is willing to give her a little time to grow up. Let's be thankful for that, Elizabeth."

Then Wynn continued, "I am more inclined, however, to think that the chief might want Kinook for a wife for his oldest son. He didn't say so directly—but I caught him looking in the young brave's direction as we talked. I wouldn't be surprised if the boy has let his wishes be known to his father."

I pictured the young brave. Come to think of it, I had seen him strutting past our campfire on more than one occasion. I was sure that Kinook, though she kept her eyes properly lowered, had seen him, too. I smiled.

"That would be nice—sometime in the future," I murmured.

"In the future," repeated Wynn. "For now let's be glad that she will be allowed to grow up."

Wynn was right. For now Kinook would have a home where she was loved and cared for. At least she would not need to be a child bride. A year was not long, but perhaps by then she would be ready to receive gifts from the young Indian brave.

Wynn told me he would send for a French translation of the New Testament for LaMeche.

"Oh, Wynn, wouldn't it be wonderful if there was a group of believers here when we return?"

Wynn smiled at my certain "when" and gave me a hug.

Chapter Twenty-five

Leaving

The day the loaded wagons and team of builders pulled laboriously into the camp was one of surprises in more than one way. I never would have guessed that the people would react so strangely. The Indian men strutted about, putting on a show of great bravery in the face of possible danger at the hands of the strange white men. Women fearfully held their ground with lowered eyes and bated breath—you could see them wishing to be able to take to the woods for protection. In fact, a few of them did just that. Many of the little children ran and hid themselves, wild with fright at the sight of all the strange-looking newcomers.

The chief, too, forced a brave front and stalked out to meet the men, but it was clear he feared placing his life in danger by doing so.

Wynn and LaMeche took charge and told the crew where to leave the wagons and tether the tired horses. Then Wynn supervised the setting up of the canvas tents and welcomed the trail-weary men to our fire for coffee to wash the dust from their parched throats.

There were nine of them in the party. All but three would be staying. The Mountie who was to take our place looked very young to me, and I wondered if it was his first posting and if he would be able to handle things if a crisis were to develop.

It is none of my business, I reminded myself. The Force must know their own men, and certainly all of them had to start someplace.

And then lovely young Kinook walked by our fire, her tall back straight, her dark hair swinging free, her head supporting a container of fresh water. And I saw the Mountie look after her, his eyes full of wonder as he nearly forgot to swallow the hot coffee in his mouth. I smiled to myself, realizing just how young he really was.

I greeted the supply wagons with mixed emotions. I knew it was best for the settlement that work begin as quickly as possible on the building of the post and the cabins. I knew there was much to be done before the coming of the winter snows. I knew also that LaMeche was anxious to have a home so he might take Silver Star to be his wife. But in spite of all those things, I also realized that in just a few days' time I would be asked to leave with those same departing wagons, and I dreaded that thought—even if our circumstances here were primitive.

The men spent the evening hours in counsel

with Chief Crow Calls Loud. He had to be consulted about his wishes for the site of the new settlement. He also, out of respect for his position, was informed about the new trading post, introduced to the young Mountie who would represent the law, and informed that Wynn and I would be leaving.

Wynn was surprised at the chief's reaction to that news. He expressed first surprise and then displeasure, asking if it was possible to revoke the decision.

"The home for Golden-Haired One can be built first," he insisted. "The chief and the people wish her to stay."

"It seems that you made quite an impression on our chief," Wynn told me with a grin. "He doesn't want to lose you."

I flushed slightly, very surprised at the turn of events. Had the villagers really been so fearful of the evil connected with the site of the impinging witch doctor that the chief was seeing in my departure a possibility that the powers could be reestablished? It was all very strange.

Silver Star stayed close to me the next day. I was glad to have her nearby. But we had very little time to talk in private.

When we went to the lake to wash the evening dishes for the last time, we were finally alone.

"I want to tell you how much—how full of joy I am to know Kinook and Kinnea will be in your home," I said to Silver Star as I swished sand around in a pot to scour the sides.

Silver Star kept her eyes lowered.

"They are like sisters to me," she said softly.

"And to me," I said, a tear rolling down each of my cheeks.

"I will miss you," I continued. "I am sorry we cannot go to your wedding."

She nodded silently.

"I hope much joy will share your path," I continued.

She looked at me then. "I will make him happy if it is in my power to do so; in that I will find joy."

Yes, I thought, that is the secret. Silver Star's love caused her to think only of the way that she could bring happiness to the man she loved. She asked nothing except that she be successful at that. Then she too would find her happiness.

Silver Star pushed aside the pot on which she was working. She looked at me and there was no shyness in her now. She regarded me evenly, her eyes not lowering as they met mine. "You will be back when summer comes again?" she asked me.

"That is what I want," I answered honestly.

"I, too, have much hope," she said in her soft, flowing voice. "Louis told me about his prayer, and I ask him to tell me more about it. I want to give honor to Louis' Great Spirit."

"Oh, Silver Star," was all I could manage right then. I wanted to hug her, but since that was not the Indian way, I squeezed her arm instead. "Someday

He be your Great Spirit too. I pray for you every day," I promised her.

"I see you pray after time of fire, like talk to a real person," Silver Star told me with wonder in her voice.

Then she said, "I wish to plant your garden. Louis has promised to help. I know not the way of the seed, but he has planted before. You will need your garden when you return."

I was deeply touched. I reached out to take Silver Star's hand. She returned my brief squeeze ever so gently.

"That would please me," I said. "I will bring you seeds."

Such a small thing—yet it brought me so much joy. When I returned—if I returned, I reminded myself—I would be coming not to a village where hostility and isolation awaited me; I would be coming back to dear friends—friends who thought of me while I was gone. Friends who welcomed me back. Friends who cared for my garden. Friends who would be ready to be introduced to the God I knew and loved. I swallowed away the tears in the back of my throat and smiled at Silver Star.

It was a sad parting the next morning at sunup. I wanted to take Silver Star and her dear babies in my arms and hold them before I bid them good-bye, but that was not the way of this people. I looked tenderly at beautiful Kinook and longed to hold her, too. Then I turned to her younger sister, Kinnea. She would be just as beautiful as her pretty sister one day soon.

I said my good-byes in the proper way, all the while aching inside. Would it really help the pain to be able to embrace them? I supposed if I could put my arms around them, I would also cry. But even crying might bring some relief.

Just as we were ready to step up into the wagon, LaMeche came. He held out his hand to Wynn and shook it firmly. Then he extended his hand to me. I took it, saying nothing but feeling so much. This hostile man whom I once feared had turned out to be my friend, my burden-sharer—and now a fellow believer!

He must have read my thoughts—or else shared them, for without a word, he stepped closer to me and gave me a generous, brotherly embrace. My breath caught in my throat and just as I expected, tears began to flow.

I was busy wiping them away when a voice from behind made me turn around. It was the chief, dressed in beaded buckskins and flowing feathers, his entourage trailing behind him. All three wives, his children, his councilors stood in their respective positions.

He approached slowly, his arms extended toward me. In his hands he held a beautiful silver fox fur.

"The chief gives gift to Golden-Haired One as token that village is her home, and we will wait for her return when meadows again bring forth their blossoms," he said.

I was deeply touched. In my confusion, I almost forgot to lower my gaze. Just in time I caught myself and dipped my head respectfully; then I stepped forward and without looking up, extended my hands.

"Great chief and his people honor me," I said in an unsteady voice. "I, too, will watch for time of meadow flowers and my return to village of my people."

Then I stepped back and Wynn helped me to climb aboard the lumbering wagon where our few belongings were piled in behind us.

The driver shouted a command to the horses, and the slow wheels started to grind forward. We were on our way.

I dared not look back. Even if it had not been a native custom to never look back when one took to the trail, I could not have done so. The tears were freely falling down my cheeks. I did not want to see the strange little campsite beside the lake. I did not want to look at those who stood there, those villagers who were now my friends—including one who was now part of our spiritual family and another who was very close to God's kingdom. I did not want to see the little area off to the side on the small island where my garden, now almost bare, had provided many meals for our fellow survivors. Nor did I want to see the charred remains of what once had been the village.

I forced myself to look ahead, to gaze at the winding trail, the rutted roadway that would lead us over the next hill, and many, many, more hills before we reached the small settlement of Athabasca Landing.

What awaits us there? I wondered. Surely it could not be better than what we now left behind.

Then I brought my thoughts under control. Did not the same God still have His hand upon me for good? In my sorrow over having to leave friends, had I forgotten that He was still traveling with me? I wiped the tears and blew my nose. Surely, if He had something better than all of this for me, it must be good indeed.

Chapter Twenty-six

Athabasca Landing

As was my custom, I walked and rode inter-changeably, partly for my own comfort and partly so I would be company for Kip.

Most of our time on the trail we had decent weather, although the mosquitoes and blackflies were hard to endure. It rained most of one day, which did not totally stop our progress, though it certainly did slow us down. I think I was as glad as the horses to stop that night.

Wynn pitched our tent under the shelter of the tall spruce and pine trees, and it looked as if we had a good chance to stay comparatively dry for the night. But in the night a strong wind came up and uprooted a tree. As it fell, one of its branches caught our tent and ripped a large tear all along the right side.

I was so thankful the tree itself hadn't fallen on us that I couldn't complain over a little rain. We did have to get up and dress and try to keep dry by wrapping the remaining piece of canvas around our-selves.

The next day it was sunny again, and as we traveled Wynn stitched the tent the best he could. The patch wasn't very attractive, but it did manage to give us some privacy on the rest of the journey.

I had given up even thinking about Athabasca Landing when we dipped over a sharp hill, and there stretched out beneath us was the shimmery ribbon of the river and the little town tucked on its south shores.

What a relief! Even in my weariness, my heart beat extra fast with excitement.

We had to cross the river by ferry. It was a large, flat barge that took one wagon at a time, horses and all. The horses were distrustful of the conveyance and snorted and plunged about, rocking our boat and causing me to nearly panic, lest they upset us midstream. It was all the drivers could do to hold the horses in check.

When at last, wagon by wagon, we docked on the other side, we set out, Wynn reading the map to our driver so he could find our new location.

It was a small settlement, but to my delight it looked quite civilized. There were shops and places of business, and even some small churches and a *school! I might enjoy my winter here after all!* I exulted.

Wynn first stopped to report to the North West Mounted Police Office and after a few minutes, came out with a large key in his hand and the directions to what would be our new home.

Pulling to a stop in front of it, I decided it was not a grand place by any means, but it was adequate. Coming from the small cabin of our past winter, to us it looked more than comfortable.

It was made of lumber and painted white, with a bit of black trim, and the windows, real windows, looked so large to me I wondered where I would ever find enough curtain material to cover them.

We entered the attached porch and passed through to a compact kitchen with its own small cupboard, a cookstove, table and chairs. Not only did it have a floor, but it also had linoleum covering the boards.

Off the kitchen was a family sitting room with a large stone fireplace and a couch and chair. A small writing table was tucked up against one wall.

Off the sitting room were *two* bedrooms! We used the largest one for our own use and set the other aside for storage or a guest room, whichever was needed. Both rooms held beds, and though the mattresses were rather lumpy, I told myself I would be spoiled in no time by such luxury.

A neat little picket fence surrounded the property and in back were three small buildings—one for storage, one for wood supply, and the third for the outside toilet.

Near the door was a well with a pump. I thought of my trips to the stream with my bucket and marveled at all the comforts of the modern world.

After exploring our new surroundings, Wynn

and the driver began to unload our wagon. We had very little to unload. We did have the things we had decided were unnecessary for survival when we moved into the tiny cabin at Smoke Lake. In the crates were some of my most treasured possessions, and I was thankful to God they had been preserved for me. If it had not been for their being crated and stored on the wagon, I was sure I no longer would have my books or the pictures of baby Samuel.

With the few things I had managed to grab before the fire, we had precious little. *But "things" don't seem nearly as important since the fire*, I thought as I looked at Wynn.

The Force had given Wynn an allowance to help purchase items we had lost in the fire. This helped greatly in establishing our new home. Wynn turned the money over to me, and I spent several days searching through the little shops, trying to find the best bargains. I had to stretch the money a long way to make us presentable again.

One of my first purchases was an old treadle sewing machine. It did not work very well, but it did manage to make a seam. With its use, and many hours of work, I was able to sew quite a number of things to help our dollars stretch.

All my dresses, my undergarments, all the curtains, towels, tea towels, cushions, potholders, and countless other articles were sewn on that old machine.

After three weeks of searching for materials and

sewing from morning to night, I finally felt that Wynn and I were really "at home." I had hardly taken the time to look beyond our doors.

Another one of my first tasks was to write lengthy letters to all our family members. It was such a long time since we had been able to write to them. Now we were where mail could be sent out and brought in with regularity, and I was anxious to let them know where and how we were.

The first Sunday we were in the town, I had nothing fit to wear to a berry patch, let alone church. Under the circumstances, Wynn suggested that we have our own worship at home as we had been doing for a number of years. I agreed, though I was anxious to attend worship services again.

The next Sunday I had a dress ready, new shoes purchased and an inexpensive hat I had found in one of the downtown stores. I was not fancy, but I felt presentable. But after walking the several blocks to the little mission, we found a note posted on the door that due to a death in the family, the parson had left town and would be gone for the following week as well. Deeply disappointed, we returned home and had our own time of worship again.

There was no use returning the third Sunday as we already knew the parson would still be away, so we fixed a picnic lunch and walked to the river where we watched the water traffic, had our lunch and then our worship time together.

Now with the fourth Sunday soon approaching, I was looking forward with all of my heart to getting together with those who shared like-faith to sing praises to the Lord and worship Him with a body of believers. And besides, I had an appropriate dress, hat and gloves just waiting to be worn to church!

I cleaned and pressed Wynn's scarlet tunic and polished my new shoes until they shone. I had put new lace on the plain hat and added a little bunch of velvet violets. It looked quite attractive when I had finished. I dug my best lace handkerchief out of the mothballs along with my woolen shawl, aired them both thoroughly to get rid of the smell, and felt that I was finally ready for the day of worship.

It was a cool day when we set off once more for the little church. I was as nervous and excited as a young girl being courted for the first time. Anxious and frightened about meeting my new neighbors, I wondered if I would still know how to act in public.

About thirty-five people gathered together for worship. Most of them were elderly women and women with young children. A few men were sprinkled among them. *Rather a morose and quiet lot*, I thought as I looked around me. *I wonder if there are any couples our age in the town.*

The church had an old upright piano that sat in one corner, but no one played to accompany the singing. My hands ached to try it. It had been so long since I had had opportunity to sit at a keyboard. I wondered if I would still be able to read the music.

The singing did not go well. The preacher himself was unable to stay on tune and the others were not sure what to sing either. It pained me to hear the dear old songs so abused.

We all stood for the reading of the Scriptures. I gloried in taking part in the congregational reading of the Word.

The parson's sermon was about "choices." "Ye cannot love God and mammon," he reminded us. "A choice has to be made." He expounded on the theme for fifty-five minutes, citing several examples—all on the "mammon" side of the issue that he had encountered in his lifetime.

I knew the preacher spoke with conviction. I knew the Word was true. I knew it was a lesson every Christian must learn and practice. But my heart felt a little heavy as I walked down the steps of the church that first day back to worship after so many years of worshiping alone in the wilderness. I had so hoped for a note of joy. I wanted to praise. I wanted to worship. I wanted to fellowship. I felt I had not been allowed to really do any of those things. I would have to wait for another whole week for joint communion. My steps were a little slower going home, but I said nothing to Wynn.

Just as we reached the gate to our little abode, he reached out and took my hand.

"After we have our dinner," he said, "would you

mind if we took our Bible and went out alone somewhere for our own little praise service again? Guess
we've done it for such a long time I have the feeling
that the day won't be complete unless we do."

I wanted to hug him. I did so need to worship.

After we had read the Scriptures and had our
time of praise and prayer, remembering especially
LaMeche and his newly discovered faith and Silver
Star as she searched for truth, we still lingered on
the banks of the Athabasca River. There was very
little traffic on this day, though I knew on some oc-
casions it was teeming with life and activity. Perhaps it too was taking the day off.

I sat dreamily, my thoughts wandering through
many things.

"Wynn," I questioned him, "do you think the rest
of the Indians at Smoke Lake will be open to the
gospel?"

"I would like to think so. They certainly have
changed a lot since the fire. They will be watching
those two very closely. And I can't believe the new
attitude of the chief. He might be very open to some
changes."

"But he is so superstitious," I said. "I'm afraid he
would just try to make God a part of his pagan worship someway."

"That's a danger, of course."

"How does one get them to understand that it is
not like that? It isn't a bunch of mumbo-jumbo—of

appeasing one deity who is the stronger to get him to take your side against the less strong?"

"I don't know."

I was silent for a few minutes, thinking over the incident when the chief called me to his fire to commend me.

"I was frightened," I admitted. "After the fire, the chief seemed to get this strange notion that I had some kind of special power. He . . . he acted so . . . so different than he had toward me before that."

"LaMeche told me about it."

"Did he also tell you that the chief presented me with a gift?"

"You mean the silver fox?"

"No, another one before you came back."

"You didn't show it to me that I remember," Wynn said, looking puzzled.

"I didn't show it to you because . . . because I couldn't keep it," I stammered.

"But that is an afront to a chief—"

"I know," I said with great feeling, "and I was afraid—afraid to give it back and yet I knew I couldn't keep it," I admitted.

"What did he do when you gave it back?"

"Well, you see, you had told me about the Indian custom of giving gifts—of how the chief gave a gift to honor a person, and that if the person didn't accept the gift, it would disgrace the chief. So I knew it might make a problem to return the gift, yet I didn't know—well, what to do about it."

"I don't follow," said Wynn. "You have totally lost me. The chief gave you a gift. You knew he would be offended if you gave it back—and yet you did."

"Well, not at first. At first I accepted it and thanked him for his kindness. I even told him that it gave me joy—and it did."

Wynn shook his head. He reached out and took my hand, giving me his lopsided grin. "My dear Elizabeth," he said, "you are talking strange riddles."

"No—" I insisted, "no riddles."

"So what was the chief's gift?"

I bit my lip to keep it from trembling. Even now, thinking about the gift brought tears to my eyes. Slowly I lifted my eyes to Wynn's. "It was his youngest son," I answered. "Nanawana's baby boy."

Wynn took my hand and squeezed it. He was silent for many minutes. When he spoke his voice was soft with emotion. "What did you do?"

I still didn't look up. "I took him, like I said. I held him for a few minutes."

Then my eyes went to Wynn's. "Oh, Wynn! He was so precious. He looked at me with those big black eyes. He didn't even look frightened. Then he sort of squirmed in my arms and smiled right at me. I could see Nanawana holding her breath in anguish. I knew how much she loved her son and what a hard thing the chief was asking of her.

"I told the chief that his gift pleased me greatly, and then I said that I wished in return to give the great chief a gift, and I . . . I gave him back his son."

"What can I say, Elizabeth," said Wynn, turning my hand over in his much larger ones. "I had no idea anything like this had happened. I'm sure it made you relive our loss of Samuel. I'm sorry, truly sorry."

I blinked away my tears.

"No wonder the chief holds you in such high esteem," Wynn went on.

"Esteem, I think I can handle," I said soberly. "Reverence—no."

"Meaning?"

"Meaning it frightened me when comments were made alluding to some strange power on my part. I don't want them to mix me up in their paganistic worship. They attribute everything to some power— good or evil. And it seems to me that good is equated with strength. Whoever wins is the one they follow."

"Yes," agreed Wynn, "they are still a very superstitious people. They have been isolated from civilization and from the truth of Christianity. Most other villages have had missionaries, trappers, extensive contact with other people, but this little village at Smoke Lake seems to have been left behind by the rest of the world."

"I pray there will be some way to reach them. Some way to make them understand the true God— on His terms."

"Perhaps—" mused Wynn, "—perhaps God has

used you to open a door for spiritual understanding."

My eyes grew wide. It was hard to believe that I could have had a part in such a glorious venture. And then I dropped my gaze again.

"I may have spoiled it," I admitted.

"Spoiled it? In what way? You said the chief accepted the gift back without offense."

"He did. But I . . . when I found that the chief thought I . . . well, that I had power of some kind, well, I decided to take advantage of it. Not for myself, but for all the people. You see, everyone—that is, all of the men except LaMeche—were just lying around camp doing nothing. And after the men came back, then the women didn't want to do anything either. It was pure chaos, with no one hunting or fishing or getting the meals for their groups or anything. Then when the chief sort of set me up, with authority, I decided to go ahead and make him listen to me. I didn't mean to take advantage of him—not at the time. But when I got to thinking about it later, that's exactly what I did.

"I went to him and told him that we had to get organized, that everyone had to work. And strangely enough, he listened and then did what I said."

I sat quietly, waiting for Wynn to say something. He said nothing.

I looked up, my lip trembling again. "I've been feeling guilty ever since I realized how it must have seemed to him," I confessed. "By going to him as I did, I as good as claimed to be what he thought me to be—someone with special powers. He never would have listened to an ordinary woman, you know that."

"And it's been bothering you?"

"Very much," I admitted, my voice faltering. "That's why I've been so touchy when anyone teased me about it. You see, I had hoped too that maybe now the villagers and the chief would be open to the salvation message. But I might have spoiled that. By taking the power and authority that didn't belong to me, I might have ruined any chance for the people to listen."

"Did you tell the chief you had special power?"

"Of course not!"

"What did you tell him?"

"I told him that I was just a woman—that I came in the name of the true God—that I—" I stopped short, struggling with emotion, and then went on. "But don't you see? That is what frightens me. I didn't mean it in that way, but I think the chief misunderstood. He seemed to think of me as . . . as some kind of sorceress or something, representing some new god. Oh, Wynn, it was like I was just a— a new witch doctor with another group or something. It frightens me. How can we make him understand the truth when he seems to have it so mixed up? And I'm the one who mixed him up," I finished lamely.

Wynn passed me his handkerchief and sat quietly for several minutes while I wiped away tears. When he felt I was under control, he spoke again.

"We'll pray, Elizabeth. You didn't mean to deceive him. You tried to explain the truth to him. When we speak the truth and someone misunderstands us, I don't believe God holds us responsible for his misinterpretation. We can't work within his mind. At least, by appearances, the chief is at a point where he has recognized another power—another god. Now someone—maybe LaMeche—needs to explain to him just who that God is and how one worships Him. You might have opened that door after all."

Chapter Twenty-seven

Involvement

The pastor came to call on us, welcoming us to his church and expressing his desire for us to be an active part of the fellowship.

"It has not been easy," he stated, "getting enough willing workers to make the church function as it ought."

"What might we do to help?" asked Wynn on behalf of both of us.

The pastor's eyes showed surprise. It had been awhile since he had had a volunteer.

He cleared his throat, seeming to find it difficult to know just where to start. "We need Sunday school teachers in the worst way," he stated. "We have some junior boys, five of them, and no teacher. Right now I fear they will stop coming if something isn't done. Two of them already have."

Wynn thought quietly, nodding his head at the pastor's words.

"We need other teachers in the children's department as well. There is only one teacher for all of the primaries. She has fourteen, from grades one

through four. They're a real handful. She's threatening to quit."

"I would love to teach some of them," I quickly
responded.

"And I would consider that group of boys," said
Wynn.

The pastor's face relaxed. Then a broad smile
began to spread across it.

"My wife will be so relieved," he said. "She's the
teacher of the primaries now. It has been such a
handful for her. She's not as young as she once was,
you know. She raised five of her own, but it's not as
easy for her to handle young ones now as it used to
be."

There was silence while the pastor wiped his
brow.

"I noticed you have a piano," I said cautiously.

The man smiled. "A piano, yes, but no pianist. It
would boost the singing so much if we had someone
to play." Then he grinned, a twinkle in his eye. "As
you could undoubtedly tell, I'm not much of a song
leader. I'm afraid the Lord neglected to give me that
gift."

He laughed, and I found myself liking the man
who tried so hard to do all he could.

I stole a glance at Wynn, wondering just how he
would respond to my announcement.

"My husband has a lovely singing voice," I said,
"and he knows almost all of the hymns."

The preacher looked from me to Wynn. Wynn

showed no signs of embarrassment or resentment.

"Would you consider—" The pastor let the words hang.

"If you feel it would be of service, I would try it," said Wynn, very simply.

"Oh, my, I would appreciate that," the man said sincerely.

Then Wynn cleared his throat and looked at me with his special grin, "And while we are announcing the talents of one another," he said, "I might inform you that my wife is a pianist."

Pastor Kelly looked at me. Now his eyes were very wide. His mouth hung open. He pulled out his handkerchief again, but this time he wiped at the corners of his eyes.

"Would you?" he asked sincerely.

"I would be happy to," I assured him.

He blew his nose rather loudly, put his handkerchief away and fumbled for words. "You folks can't appreciate what this means to me—and to Martha. We sort of struggled along here—and it's been tough going. We served in larger parishes before, but we felt the Lord wanted us to give some of our years of service to a mission. I . . . think perhaps we did it backward. We should have spent our years in a mission first and then gone to a larger parish.

"Anyway, it has been hard for us. Especially for Martha. Wait until she hears the news. You see, we've been praying for some time now—"

He stopped and cleared his throat. Then he

looked up with glistening eyes. "Well," he said, "one should not be so surprised when God answers. Just thankful. Just thankful."

My own eyes felt a little misty, so I decided it was time to serve the tea and cake.

After the good parson had left us, Wynn and I reviewed our commitments of the past hour. It would be so good to be involved in the life of the church again, we both decided. We had missed it.

"I need to go over to the church and get in a little practice on that piano," I said. "It has been so long since I have played that I'm sure I'm quite rusty."

"Bring a hymnbook home with you if you can," Wynn said, "and we'll pick out the Sunday hymns together."

"I'm going to love teaching children again," I mused, thinking about the small minds and their interest in the Bible stories. It had been several years since I'd had the privilege.

Wynn just smiled. "Well, since you're so enthusiastic, I might give you my junior boys and I'll take your little people," he said laughingly. "Do you know what junior boys can be like?"

"I do. And I'm sure you will make out just fine."

"You heard the pastor. Some of them have already dropped out. I'm guessing the rest of them are looking for an excuse too."

"Don't forget," I reminded Wynn. "They have never had a man for a teacher. I'm sure you'll win them over in no time—just wait and see."

"I hope you're right, Elizabeth, but I wouldn't count on junior boys being quickly 'won over' by anyone."

I patted Wynn's shoulder. "Just wait," I said with total confidence. "You'll see."

The truth was I could hardly wait to start teaching, and deep down under his banter, I was sure Wynn felt the same way.

I had a caller the next morning. When I answered the door, a small, carefully dressed lady stood on the step. I smiled a welcome and opened the door.

"Mrs. Delaney," she said, "I do hope this isn't an imposition. I'm Martha Kelly and I wanted to bring the Sunday school material for you and your husband."

"Oh, yes. It's so nice to meet you, Mrs. Kelly," I said, extending my hand. "Please come in."

I led Mrs. Kelly to our small but cozy sitting room and took her coat. She retrieved the bundle she had brought with her and lifted out a small package.

"I brought you a bit of baking," she said rather shyly, "as a welcome to our church and little town."

It had been so long since anyone had welcomed me in such a way. I was delighted. I expressed my thanks to Mrs. Kelly and excused myself to put on the teakettle.

She showed me the Sunday school material and

explained how the classes would be divided and where my room would be found and then we chatted about other things.

She was a delightful lady! It would be so nice to have a friend—a warm and understanding friend.

I went to the church the next day to practice the piano. I knew I would be rusty and fumbling. The first few tries were frustrating, but I was surprised at how quickly it all came back to me. Soon I was enjoying the sound of the hymns of praise.

The piano was understandably out of tune, but it was not horribly so. I decided that Wynn would have no problem leading the singing to its accompaniment.

The pastor came out of his study just as I was about to leave the church. I apologized for disturbing him. I realized, too late, that I should have checked before I began to play.

"It was not a disturbance," he assured me. "It was a ministry. I needed that music to lift my soul. I am sure my Sunday sermon will be the better for it."

I asked about taking home a hymnal for Wynn and me to pick the hymns. He assured me I was most welcome.

I asked for the theme of his Sunday sermon, and he said he planned to speak on the surety of God's promises. I could hardly wait for Sunday.

I was beginning to settle into our new little community. After I had done all of my sewing and arranged our small house, I could not find enough to do to fill my days. The hours until Wynn came home often weighed on me. I was sure there were things I could be doing to serve this small community if I could just discover what they were.

I still had not become very acquainted with neighbors. In fact, where our house stood we had few neighbors. To our right was a large vacant lot and beyond it was the property belonging to the North West Mounted Police. Their small office was located there as well as storage sheds, wagon yards and barns.

Wynn was so close that he could come home for his noon meal, which helped to fill my day. It was a great pleasure for me to be able to see so much of my husband after his being gone all day and sometimes many days at a time.

Wynn settled into the routine of office work. I knew it was a very different life than he was used to, and I am sure he sometimes chafed under the load of paper work, but he did not complain. He seemed to like the two young men who served under him, and that certainly helped his circumstances.

The two-month sentence of the young brave from the village expired and Wynn had his horse, which also had been kept in custody, brought to him. Wynn also saw to it that he had provisions for the long ride home. I sent a letter for LaMeche to read to Silver

Star. Then Wynn escorted the boy a day's ride out of town to make sure he wouldn't come into possession of illegal whiskey again; and bidding him good-bye and a safe journey, he sent him on his way.

When I asked Wynn if he felt the young man had learned a lesson, he smiled.

"I think he has learned several lessons, Elizabeth," he said: "how to play blackjack, how to chew tobacco, how to curse in English, and who knows what else."

I cringed at Wynn's words. Though he spoke partly in jest, I knew there was truth in it.

As for me, I was getting acquainted with the shopkeepers in the town, though I still knew few of them by name. Most of the shopkeepers were men, but there was a woman working in the drygoods store and one in the bakeshop.

Our home was small but adequate, our town was scattered but interesting, our church was struggling but growing, and though we both missed the life with the Indian people, we settled in to enjoy this one winter set apart.

We talked about and prayed often for the village we had left in the fall. We hoped with all our heart that the building was going well, that the young Mountie was able to care for the needs of the people, and that the Force would see fit to return us to the posting in the spring. We also prayed that the gospel witness in that town would take root and grow.

Mail from the South arrived. Wynn brought the letters home to me when he came for lunch one day. There were four of them: one from Mary, one from Julie, one from my mother, and one from Mother Delaney.

There was both good news and bad news. The war was finally over and Matthew had returned home safely. I thanked God fervently. Matthew was now busy learning the business to take over from Father.

Julie's baby boy had arrived. He had been a healthy baby until he was five months old, at which time he had contracted measles with complications and he had gone home to God. Julie had been heartbroken, but God had been with her and her husband. They were now expecting a second child.

My tears fell uncontrollably as I thought of my dear, light-hearted sister and her deep sorrow. I thanked God her letter held no bitterness, only love for her young preacher husband and faith in her mighty God.

Jon and Mary's family were keeping well, though Elizabeth, their climber, had suffered a broken arm in a fall from a ladder left beside the house. The arm had healed nicely, and they hoped she had learned a lesson.

Mother Delaney had had two more hospital stays, one resulting in gall-bladder surgery. Now she was feeling much better. Phillip and Lydia's family were all well and growing.

I read each letter over many times before I laid them aside. It was the next best thing to a good visit with those we loved.

Chapter Twenty-eight

Service

I was excited with my new Sunday school class—even more excited than I was about the opportunity to again play the piano. I was given a class of six energetic seven- and eight-year-olds. Four of them were girls and two were boys.

One of the boys, a real handful, had been raised by a man who had lost his wife in childbirth. He had chosen, in his bitterness, not to remarry. I'm afraid his wrath affected his growing son. It was a neighbor lady who somehow managed to get Willie to Sunday school. The father had no room in his life for God, but the woman's son was the only friend of the young boy and so the two came to Sunday school together.

They could not have been more different. Stephen Williams was a quiet, small-framed boy with a lisp and questioning blue eyes. He had learned not to speak unless spoken to. I think it had to do with being ridiculed by other children rather than because of good manners.

Willie Schultz, on the other hand, was big for his

age, loud and cantankerous, never stopped talking, and had a quick and fiery temper to go with his shock of unruly reddish hair.

They seemed such an unlikely pair to be "best friends," but it was evident to me from the first Sunday that they considered themselves just that.

They insisted on sitting together, sharing a book, that they be separated from "the girls," and that they be allowed to communicate whenever they wished.

I, on the other hand, insisted that they sit across the room from one another, each have his own book, be intermingled with the girls and be quiet unless I asked them to speak.

For a few moments it seemed as if I would be the loser. They looked glumly at one another, threatening to "never come again," Willie's rage showing in his eyes, but as the lesson went on they got involved and forgot to continue their protest.

Thankfully, all four of my girls were quite well behaved. I learned that one, called Mary, was the daughter of the lady in the bakeshop. She was a bit on the tubby side—*she must have free hand in sampling the goods*, I decided.

Molly and Polly were twins, daughters of the town's blacksmith, and Sue Marie was the daughter of the man who worked on the ferry boat. I later learned that Sue Marie and her family had lived in many places, her father shifting from job to job. For this reason Sue Marie had had very little education.

She would just be starting classes at one school and they would be on the road again, often to places where there was no school. Sunday school was a new experience for Sue Marie as well, and it was because of the kindnesses of Mrs. Kelly to the family that Sue Marie was allowed to attend.

So I looked at my Sunday school class as a great challenge. Here were six students who needed to know the truths from God's Word. For some of them, this might well be their only opportunity. I prayed for the help of the Lord.

Wynn began his class with a group of four reluctant and withdrawn boys. The first Sunday he was discouraged with their actions and their response, but much to his surprise all four were back the following Sunday.

He took them on a backpacking trip the next Saturday. Over the open fire they cooked the fish they had caught, and Wynn taught them some of the skills of survival in the wilderness. The next Sunday there were six boys in his class, and the following Sunday he had eight, all eager to get in on the activities if not to learn, and pressing for his attention.

Wynn followed the backpacking trip with canoeing and hiking. One Saturday was even spent showing how to properly start training a puppy. The puppy belonged to Jock MacGregor, and all the boys then clamored for a dog of their own so they too could get involved. I knew that when Revva's litter arrived, we would have more trainers than we had puppies.

Wynn enjoyed his "boys" and they took to dropping by our house in the evenings or on Saturday and Sunday afternoon. I often felt like I was running a restaurant for hungry youngsters, but it was fun and I never objected.

My class, too, felt welcome at our house. We spent some Saturdays baking cookies or making candy. Even the boys took part, though they were much better at eating than baking. We went for nature walks together. I promised them that when the snow was deep enough, I would teach them how to walk with snowshoes, and they were all eager to try.

With the activity of our classes and the dropping in of our students, my days were soon full. It was like having a great big family of our own.

Not all of our "family" listened well to our instructions. Willie, though he never missed Sunday school and came to the house oftener than any of my other students, still seemed to carry a chip on his shoulder. He was often belligerent and unyielding, and sometimes flew into a rage if things didn't go his way.

I tried to understand him and his needs, but I also had to be quite firm. In spite of the fact that Willie was a boy who needed lots of love and attention, I felt he also needed strong discipline to help him grow up to be of use to himself and society.

Wynn had two boys who were also a problem.

One was from a home with no resident father. His father had gone away, leaving the home and the family, and no one seemed to know where. The second one was the youngest of a brood of twelve, very needy and excessively transient. They stayed in one place only long enough to completely wear out their welcome and then moved on.

Only two of the twelve were not still living at home, though many of them were of an age to be considered adults. They stayed with the family group, clinging to one another—not out of love, however. Continual inner strife often resulted in horrible fights, with fists, or knives or anything they could get their hands on. That family was Wynn's greatest source of distress. The police force probably answered more calls to that one ramshackled home than to any other area under their patrol.

Wynn feared the young boy would grow up to follow the same wayward path as the rest of his kin. So he tried to spend time with the boy and encourage him in any way he could. The boy's name was Henry Mayers, but the kids at school all called him "Rabid," a nickname he seemed quite pleased with.

Because of all the time we were spending with our Sunday school classes, Wynn and I found that we were not getting much time to ourselves or to becoming acquainted with other people our age. We discussed it and decided we would have to set aside one night a week, informing our students we were unavailable that night. We would use that time to cultivate friendships of our own.

It didn't work out too well. There always seemed to be one child or another standing at our door with a problem to solve or a joy to share. We finally decided we would save Sunday dinner for inviting couples or families in, and the rest of the time we would be available to our class members.

I had two mothers approach me about giving piano lessons to their children, and, with the permission of the kind pastor, we used the church piano. I began by teaching three lessons a week. More mothers were soon calling and the lessons increased to eleven per week. There would have been more, but I felt that was all I could handle.

Our lives were busy, our days so full, that it caught me quite by surprise when it started snowing. Winter was with us again, and I hadn't even had time to anticipate or dread its coming.

Chapter Twenty-nine

Winter

This was a very different winter than I had been used to. Instead of hauling wood and melting water to keep my fire going and wash my laundry, I was teaching piano lessons to prim little girls and baking cookies for hungry boys.

My physical labor was much easier, but my days were much busier. I couldn't believe how full our life was. I was seeing less of Wynn now than when we lived at one of the villages. Even our Sundays were full, the day of the week we had previously guarded jealously for one another.

Revva's puppies arrived—five of them—but I was much too busy to help in their training. Besides, all Wynn's Sunday school boys were clamoring to help him and I knew it was important to them.

We took on the enjoyable task of taking turns having all the families of our students in for Sunday dinner. A few found some nice way to decline our invitation, but most of them accepted, and I was kept busy preparing meals both affordable and tasty.

The students each were given a written

invitation to carry home with them, inviting his or her family to our house for dinner two weeks hence. The next Sunday they were to carry back the reply. We could have asked the parents ourselves, but we wanted the students to feel part of the process. They took such delight in carrying the envelope home.

When it was Willie's turn to carry home his invitation, he looked at me with angry eyes. As it turned out, he was not angry with me.

"Why bother?" he fumed. "My old man wouldn't come."

"Perhaps you should take home the invitation and let him decide," I coaxed Willie.

"Won't do no good. He's so ugly mean. He'll just get mad and take a swing at me."

I couldn't believe one so young could be so disrespectful and mistrustful of his father.

"I'll deliver the invitation myself if you'd rather," I told Willie.

He shoved the invitation deep into his pocket. "Might swing at you, too," he growled.

I let the matter drop and went on with the class.

I decided Willie might need a little help in encouraging his father, so I did not wait for the next Sunday when Willie would bring back his reply to the invitation. Instead, I dressed in my best on Tuesday morning and headed for the small local hotel that Willie's father owned.

When I entered the building I approached the man at the desk, pleased that I would not have to ask for Mr. Schultz. His swatch of reddish hair told me where Willie got his, and a brisk, friendly mustache twitched as though in amusement when he talked. His name was pinned to the front of his striped vest, G. W. Schultz.

I smiled warmly.

"Mr. Schultz," I said, extending my hand. "I am Mrs. Delaney. It is a pleasure to make your acquaintance."

He took my hand and shook it thoroughly, murmuring something about the pleasure being all his.

"I am here to invite you to my house for dinner a Sunday from next," I continued. "I assume that you have already received a written invitation, but I wanted to make it a personal invitation as well."

"That is most kind," said Mr. Schultz.

"We will be dining at one o'clock and you are most welcome to come a few minutes before that time if you wish. However, we don't get home until around twelve-thirty from our morning church service."

"That sounds lovely," said Mr. Schultz, giving me a big smile, his mustache twitching.

He certainly seems friendly enough, I thought to myself. *Why do people paint him as such an ogre?*

I got even more daring.

"It would be delightful to have you join us for the morning service if you are free."

"I just might do that," said Mr. Schultz.

I felt ecstatic. Never had I been received so graciously.

"We will count on that then," I said, and gave the man one of my nicest smiles.

"Certainly. And I thank you for your kindness. I shall look forward to the Sunday after next."

I turned to go and then turned back again, with what I hoped was a winning smile, "Mr. Schultz," I said rather teasingly, yet meaningfully, "you don't have to wait for two weeks to attend our church, you know. You would be most welcome anytime—even next Sunday."

He twirled his long reddish mustache, "Mrs. Delaney," he said, "I have never had a more pleasant invitation."

I flushed slightly and fumbled with the doorknob. Just as I was about to make my exit, he spoke again.

"Mrs. Delaney," he said, "please don't take offense, but are you a widow, ma'am?"

I turned back, my face warming under his gaze.

"No . . . no . . . of course not."

"Then might I ask just why you are asking a bachelor like myself to dinner?"

"The invitation explained that, I—"

"What invitation?"

"Why the one your son—"

"My son? I have no son. As I said, I am a bachelor, Mrs. Delaney."

My gloved hand flew to my face.

"But Willie, my Sunday school pupil—"

The man began to laugh. His roar shook the building. I saw nothing funny about the situation. He didn't even explain it really, just pointed to a door, and said, "In there. That's who you wish to see—my brother."

It was a bad start all around. By the time I knocked on the door, I was already flustered and embarrassed. When he answered the knock, I opened the door and stepped in.

The room was an office. The desk in front of the man was piled high with accounts and books. He didn't even look up but growled at me, "Yeah?"

I cleared my throat to begin.

"Excuse me, sir."

His head jerked up at the sound of my voice. He scowled at me as though I had some nerve to come interrupting his work.

He had the same shock of reddish hair, the same bushy mustache, only his did not twitch with amusement. It bristled with indignation. His eyes pinned me to the spot.

I wanted to get out of there. The only way I could see to do so was to speak my piece quickly and then retreat.

I wanted no misunderstandings. I started by clarifying my position.

"I am Mrs. Delaney," I said in what I hoped was an even voice. "My husband is the new commander at the North West Mounted Police Post. I am Willie's

Sunday school teacher. I understand you are Willie's father?"

There was silence for a few moments. I began to think he wasn't even going to answer me; then he threw down the pencil he was working with and gave me a withering look.

"So what's he done now?"

"Done? Why, nothing. I . . . I . . ."

He glared at me.

"If he hasn't done anything, what are you doing here?"

"I came to personally follow up the invitation I sent home with your son last Sunday."

He stood to his feet. He was a tall man, stockily built. I could see why a child would find him intimidating.

"What invitation?" he snapped. "One to your little Sunday school class?" he actually sneered as he asked the question. "Now look here, Miss Whatever your name is"—he left his chair and came around his desk where he could stand glowering down on me—"they asked for my kid to go to that there church. I'm not for it, but I didn't think it could do no harm; besides, it gets him out of my hair for a few hours. Sunday morning is the only time I get to sleep. Now you got the kid; what more do you want?"

I was angry. I was frightened. I was trembling with inner rage. How could this overgrown child be acting so foolishly? *It must run in the family!* I fumed. First his—his humorous brother allowed me to make a complete fool of myself, and now he had the nerve to stand over me as though shaking a finger at a naughty school child, all because I happened to care about his son!

I stepped back, not to get away from him, but so I could get a good look at his angry red face and his snapping eyes.

"Excuse me, Mr. Schultz," I said. "I think you have a few things confused here. In the first place, I am not inviting you into my Sunday school class. I do not allow spoiled, cantankerous children to take a part. And second, I was here to invite you to our home for Sunday dinner, not because I feel that your presence will be particularly enjoyable but because I happen to care about your son.

"No, Mr. Schultz, Willie has not 'done something,' but he will someday if you don't give him more of your time and love. He needs a parent— now! We at the church love him and are trying to help him to grow up to be a God-fearing, law-abiding citizen, but we can't do it alone. Willie is already hostile—and he's not going to reform unless *you* do."

The face before me was changing. There was first a look of such anger that I thought he might strike me, and then there was a look of absolute unbelief. I was sure no one, at least no one in his right mind, had ever addressed him the way I had. I still wasn't through.

"And finally, Mr. Schultz," I said, "I am willing to

guess that Willie had a mother who was an upright, decent woman, and it would bring her great pain if her son did not grow up to be a decent man."

I stopped and took a breath. My words were beginning to catch up with me and in shame and embarrassment I mumbled to a halt. My face flushed, and tears that I had stubbornly refused threatened to appear. I lowered my face.

"I'm sorry," I stammered. "I apologize for my outburst. I had no reason to act in such a rude manner. It's inexcusable. Forgive me, please."

I stepped around the big man who had not moved out of my way and reached with a trembling hand for the doorknob. I needed to escape.

I hesitated just long enough to say in not much more than a whisper, "The invitation still stands. A week from Sunday." I opened the door and hurried out of the office.

I would have fled to the street, but as I passed the desk where the other Mr. Schultz still worked a crossword puzzle, he looked up with a twitching mustache and twinkling eyes and said, "Bully for you."

I gave him a stony look and continued out, fighting hard to preserve some dignity.

As I reached the door, he called after me. "By the way, does my invitation still stand, too?"

Without answering him, I pulled the door open, closed it securely behind me, and kept right on going. I could hear his uproarious laughter following me.

Chapter Thirty

Sunday Dinners

The next Saturday I was at the church rehearsing with some of the junior girls for a part in the Sunday school Christmas program. Suddenly the door burst open and Willie came flying in. Without even waiting to remove his hat or take a breath, he rushed at me, his hand outstretched.

He couldn't speak, he was too out of breath. He just poked the strange piece of paper at me and urged me to take it.

I reached out and took it while he waited, breathless as I opened it on the spot.

It was a simple note, expressing only that on behalf of his son Willie and himself, Mr. Schultz would be happy to accept my invitation for Sunday dinner. I gasped and Willie looked at me with a grin on his face, his red hair flopping across his forehead.

"Why, Willie," I said, giving him a hug, "that is wonderful!"

"Told ya, he'd come," panted the boy.

"I'm so pleased," I said honestly.

"Gotta show Stephen," Willie said and was gone again.

I stood watching him, wondering what had changed the mind of the senior Schultz. Surely Willie's uncle was not playing another trick on me. No, I told myself, even he wouldn't be that heartless.

I turned back to my girls. Even our song seemed to go better, and when I left the church I walked through the lightly falling snow with a lighter step.

Maybe, just maybe, something had jolted the father to make him realize that he had a son who needed him.

Our Sunday with the Schultzes went very well. Mr. Schultz did not join us at church like I had hoped, but he and Willie arrived promptly at one o'clock.

To my relief Wynn and Mr. Schultz visited very easily and he proved to be an intelligent and even agreeable man.

Nothing was said about my visit to the hotel or my outburst. Nor was anything said about the brother who enjoyed his teasing. I wondered if Willie's father even knew of that part of the incident.

I served the dinner, letting Willie help me in the kitchen. He was pleased to pour his own milk and put on the rolls, butter, and pickles. I glanced at Mr. Schultz once or twice to see if he might object to his son doing "woman's work," but he seemed to not even notice.

It turned out that Mr. Schultz was very interested in the work of the Force. He asked several questions and Wynn was happy to answer them. They chatted amicably until I announced the meal was ready.

Mr. Schultz acted cordial enough at the table, evidencing fine table manners, even when Wynn said the table grace. The talk was light and friendly and after coffee and dessert, which I let Willie help serve, they visited a bit more; then he thanked me politely and left.

I took a big breath after I closed the door. Before I tackled the dirty dishes I turned to Wynn. "Well," I asked, "what do you think?"

"Pleasant enough man. Certainly nobody's fool," Wynn responded.

"Except where Willie is concerned," I murmured. "I'm afraid the man knows very little about the needs of a growing boy."

I turned to the dishes then, musing as I washed them. Wynn came to take a towel for drying them.

"If I help with the dishes, Mrs. Delaney," he proposed, "will you promise to go for a walk with me?"

"Is that a request or an order, Sergeant?" I teased back.

"A request," Wynn stated. "If you turn down my request, then it becomes an order."

We laughed together and hurried with the dishes so we could get our walk in.

We took Kip with us. He bounded ahead, loving

his freedom to run. He did not enjoy being confined to our fenced-in yard even if there was plenty of room.

It was a lovely winter afternoon and the fresh, crisp snow crunched underfoot as we walked.

"Just think," I remarked to Wynn. "In just three weeks it will be Christmas again."

"Are you looking forward to it?" he asked.

"I am," I admitted. "I really am. It will seem more like Christmas this year. There will be the Christmas program for the Sunday school, the church service, a tree, decorations, even a turkey for dinner. I think I will really enjoy having an old-fashioned, honest-to-goodness Christmas again."

"I'm looking forward to it, too," stated Wynn. "I'm tired of giving you new stockings."

We both laughed heartily and walked on through the downy falling snow.

Sue Marie and her family were the last students we would have in for dinner before Christmas. After Christmas we would begin asking Wynn's class members. Already we had asked each other what we would do when it came time to ask the family of Henry "Rabid" Myers. We pushed the problem into the future, vowing to cross that bridge when the time came.

Sue Marie accepted our invitation, but her family did not come with her. I was sorry we were not going to have the opportunity to meet them but promised myself that after Christmas I would at least try to get to know her mother.

With solemn, sober face, Sue Marie sat quietly and sedately in a chair while I got the meal on the table. Wynn tried to entertain her, but she only shook her head yes or no to his questions.

At the table she ate very little, though her eyes took in everything. She looked uncomfortable and shy. The apple pie she did like, and even accepted a second piece.

I didn't want to shoo her off home as soon as we had finished, so I suggested she might want to look at some books while I washed the dishes. She took the books and studied the pictures, but she didn't attempt to read them. I wondered if Sue Marie could read at all.

After I had finished with the dishes, I went in and sat down beside the little girl.

"Would you like to hear the story?" I asked. She seemed hesitant, but finally nodded her head. I was surprised at her reluctance. She had not been so shy the many times that she had been in our home with the other children. I picked up the book and began to read. Before long she was totally engrossed in the story.

We read book after book together and then she looked at the clock.

"I've got to go," she said. "Mommy said to be home by three."

I found her coat and mittens and helped her on with her boots.

She turned at the door and said politely, "Thank you for the good dinner, Miz Delaney."

"You are most welcome," I answered her. "I'm so glad you came."

She turned then to pat Kip who had bounded up to get some attention. Kip always made sure he got in on the party when the children came to the house.

Then she turned soberly to me. "Did I be good enough, Miz Delaney?" she asked, her eyes big and questioning.

"Why, you were just fine," I said kneeling beside her and putting an arm around her.

"Good," she said seriously. " 'Cause Mamma said if she heard that I don't be good, I'd get one awful spanking when I get home."

"When I see your mamma," I told her, "I'll tell her what a well-behaved little girl she has."

She broke into a big grin, and then she was gone, tripping through the winter afternoon.

The church was packed for the Sunday school Christmas program. I was responsible for all the singing and had rehearsed with the children for several Saturdays prior to the big event.

Most of our numbers were done as a group, but the twins were singing "Away in a Manger," and Willie, who I discovered had a lovely boyish tenor, sang a solo, "O Little Town of Bethlehem." Though I hoped his father would come to hear him, I didn't hazard another trip to the hotel with an invitation.

Pastor Kelly's face beamed as he welcomed the large group to the little church. From my spot at the piano, I looked over the crowd, too, spotting many parents of our students. Much to my amazement, not only was Willie's father there, but his uncle as well. The latter caught my eye and twitched his mustache in amusement before I quickly turned away.

We had only one calamity—apart from a few little mishaps, that is. When Ralph Conners, one of the shepherds from Wynn's class, turned to leave the stage, his foot caught Joseph's robe and toppled him right over before he could free his foot. Joseph's crook, Mrs. Belasky's cane, tumbled to the floor with a loud clatter, and Joey's mother's towel that he wore as a turban toppled off his head.

Joseph picked himself up, mumbling threats under his breath, plunked his headpiece haphazardly on his head partly covering one eye, and went on with his speech. The audience tittered a bit, but the play went on.

I enjoyed the evening. It was wonderful to be part of the Christmas celebration again.

As we had planned, after Christmas we started on our invitations to Wynn's class members. We didn't get quite the enthusiastic response we had gotten from my younger children. Still, we were pleased at the number of families who accepted our invitation to Sunday dinner.

The last family belonged to Henry "Rabid" Myers. Again we discussed what we should do. I took a deep breath.

"Well," I said, "the Lord Jesus loves Henry too. We invited the families of all the others—I guess that means Henry's family, too."

"That means twelve people, Elizabeth."

I nodded.

"Twelve big people."

I sighed.

"Twelve, big, mean people," teased Wynn.

"Oh, Wynn," I wailed, "don't make it any worse than it is. I'm scared enough already."

"You don't have to do it," reminded Wynn.

"I think we should."

"Okay. Then I'll give you all the help I can."

So the invitation went out to the entire Myers family, and I held my breath wondering what would happen.

Henry brought the answer the following Sunday. It was not on paper—it was by word of mouth. They said, "Sure."

Oh, my, I thought. *Oh, my.*

And then I reminded myself I had served nearly that many day after day around an open fire at the camp. I had had only vegetables and wild meat to do it with too. Why did "civilization" make things seem so much more difficult? I began planning my dinner.

I was determined to have plenty to eat—it might not be fancy, but there would be enough. I could not imagine anything more embarrassing than to have all those hearty appetites and not enough food. I dug out my largest kettle, had Wynn bring home some even bigger ones from the Force supply room and cooked in great quantities.

I had planned for twelve, the ten children who were reportedly still living at home and two parents, but when they arrived there were only ten. They all looked rather young so I assumed that the father and mother had not been able to make it.

"I'm sorry your father and mother were unable to come," I said to the girl who stood closest to me.

"Ma's been dead and gone fer years," she informed me with no seeming emotion. "Pa wasn't feeling up to it—"

"Got hisself too drunk last night," cut in one of the boys. "Can't even walk this mornin'."

He laughed, obviously thinking it a great joke.

"Sure smells good," said one of the others.

With a bit of doing, we got them all around the table. Wynn had warned me that we might have some trouble holding them back while we said the blessing, so I had planned ahead. I didn't put the food on the table. But my strategy didn't work too well. They looked around the table the moment they were seated, and then one fellow cried out, "Lizzie, get on up and make yerself useful. Food's not on yet."

We did manage to have prayer, and then all dug in. Now and then during the meal someone would say some snapping remark to one of the other ones. I was afraid at one point that a fight might break out over who was to get the first dibs on a third serving of potatoes, but they got it worked out someway and the meal went on.

When they had finished they got up, wiped their mouths on already dirty sleeves and headed for the door. There was nothing said about the meal, except for one girl who stopped momentarily and said, "Pa's sure gonna be some mad he missed it." Then with a chuckle among themselves, they left us.

Henry stood at the door for just a moment, looking ill at ease and confused and then he hurried after them.

I washed all the dirty dishes, scrubbed at the mammoth pots and tidied up the kitchen. There wasn't too much food left to put away—hardly enough to make a meal for Wynn and me the next day.

Wynn was taking apart our makeshift extension to the table as I finished the last of the kitchen chores. I took my leftover vegetables and meat to the shelf in the porch that acted as my cold storage.

Well, at least I have an extra pumpkin pie, I told myself. With a total of only twelve rather than fourteen for dinner, I had cut only three of the four. We would enjoy the pumpkin pie the next day.

I placed the dishes of leftover food on the shelf, my mind still on that tasty pie. In fact, I was tempted to cut just a sliver and have it with coffee. I figured I had earned it after serving so many and doing all those dirty dishes.

I looked about in unbelief. My pie was nowhere to be seen. And then the truth hit me like a blow.

"Wynn," I cried out, "those Myers have stolen my pie!"

Three days later the word came through the police office. The Myers had left town. A number of small items that had belonged to neighbors and businesses seemed to have left town along with them.

My heart ached for Henry. What chance was the boy to have? I prayed earnestly for him. At first he might have attended Wynn's class because he heard about the hikes and the canoe trips and the fishing, but I had hoped that he now came out of respect for Wynn. He knew that Wynn cared about him—perhaps the first person in his life who truly did.

Two nights later we were reading on one of those rare quiet evenings at home when there was a knock on our door. Wynn went to answer it and much to his amazement, Henry stood outside, shivering in the frigid night air.

Wynn hurried him in and I busied myself finding the boy something to eat. We asked no questions, but after Henry had eaten, he picked up his thin coat, mumbled his thanks, and headed for our door.

"Where are you going?" Wynn asked.

He hesitated to answer. Wynn decided to take another approach.

"I understood all your family had left town. Did they come back?"

He just shook his head.

"How did you get back then?" Wynn asked him.

He looked down uncomfortably and picked at the sleeve of his coat. "I didn't go," he finally offered. "When they said that they were goin', I ran out an' hid. They called around for a while an' then they just gave up an' left without me."

"So you are alone?"

He nodded.

"Where are you staying?"

"I was gonna stay in the house, but today some guys came an' boarded it all up, an' I can't get in."

"So you have no place?"

"I'll make out," he said, suddenly taking on a tough stance.

Wynn looked at me across the head of the young boy and I nodded in agreement.

"Tell you what," Wynn said, "we have that extra bedroom with no one in it. Why don't you just stay here?"

Henry looked too frightened to even talk.

" 'Course," said Wynn, "we'd expect you to work for your board. You'd need to carry wood and haul water. We'd also expect you to go to school every day."

The boy still said nothing.

"In return, you'd get your clothes and your meals. Mrs. Delaney is a pretty good cook. Is it a deal?" asked Wynn.

Henry shuffled his feet. I had the feeling he was trying hard to keep a smile from appearing.

"Guess so," he answered.

"Might as well take your coat off and pull up to the fire then. Maybe we could talk Mrs. Delaney into making some popcorn."

The grin finally came in spite of Henry's reluctance.

Chapter Thirty-one

Answers

At first it seemed strange to have a young boy in the house. There were many things to do. Wynn had to report the whereabouts of the child and seek temporary legal custody so we could keep him.

I had to shop for clothes and make arrangements at the local school for consultation to determine the grade in which he should be placed. His attendance had been so sporadic before that they had not even attempted to place him.

I worked with him in the evenings to help him catch up to his age group, but even though he was bright enough and we worked hard, I knew it would be some time before he was where he should have been.

He loved Kip and coaxed to have the dog share his room. As Kip was used to being in the house in the cold winter, I gave in rather readily. I did insist that Kip's place be on the rug beside the bed rather than on the bed, and when we checked the room at night after the two had retired, Henry always slept with one hand resting on the dog, his fingers curled in the heavy fur.

He was quick to learn his assigned tasks and thankfully proved not to be lazy. He carried wood and water with no prompting from me, and even looked for additional jobs to do, knowing that it would bring our praise.

The calendar was quickly using up the winter months, and I looked forward to spring with mixed emotions. I knew it could mean we would be returning to the village. I longed to go. I missed our Indian friends. I had been praying daily that God would somehow open the door so we could return and help to share the good news of Christ's coming to earth to live and die for mankind. *How can they believe on Him in whom they have not heard*, I kept asking myself? How could they know that the evil they feared could be overcome through acceptance of God's great plan of salvation?

And yet when I thought about going back to the Indian people, I also thought of my Sunday school class. They, too, needed to know about Christ and His love. I thought about Willie's father who had lived in deep bitterness for so many years and now appeared to be slowly moving out of his self-exile. I thought about Wynn's boys and their need of making that personal commitment to the Lord Jesus. If we went, would there be anyone to teach them?

But more than all that, I thought about Henry, our little deserted waif. Who would care for Henry?

Wynn and I talked about it many times, but with no conclusion. We kept putting it off. I don't think either of us wanted to face the thought of giving up the boy. It was so much easier to push the decision off into the future.

At last, one mid-April day when the spring sun was pouring its warmth upon the hillsides, causing little rivulets to run trickling toward the groaning Athabasca River as it tried to free itself from her winter ice, we knew we needed to face squarely the question: What about Henry?

"He's trying so hard and he has come so far," I maintained.

Wynn agreed, though we both knew Henry still had many things to work through.

"I'm afraid if he faces another change right now, he might regress," I continued.

"Do you suppose Stephen's folks would take him?" proposed Wynn.

"They are a fine young couple, but I'm not sure they can handle their own," I stated quite honestly. "I feel that the girls are totally undisciplined. Henry still needs a very strong hand, and Stephen's father doesn't get involved at all, and his mother is not able to follow through."

"You're right," Wynn agreed. "That is exactly the way I see them."

"What about the Kellys?" I asked.

"Do you think that would be fair? After all, they are not young anymore. They are looking forward to retirement—not raising another family."

"I suppose it would be an imposition," I reluctantly agreed.

"I wonder if Phillip and Lydia would take him?" pondered Wynn.

"Don't forget they have added another two young ones to their own family in the last few years," I reminded him. "Lydia might have all that she can handle." I paused for a moment and then said thoughtfully, "Do you suppose Jon and Mary might be willing—?"

"I don't think Henry would like city life at all. He wouldn't fit in there. The school system—William and his friends? It would be a very difficult adjustment."

"Wynn," I said, "couldn't we take him with us to the village?"

"What about his education?"

"I could get the books and teach him."

"Yes, I suppose you could. But do you really think it would be the best for him? I mean, he wouldn't know the language, wouldn't fit in with the other boys. I think he needs more support than that, Elizabeth. And you know how much I need to be gone. You'd have so much of the care of him."

We both were quiet as we thought about it. It didn't seem like the Indian village was the right place for the boy.

"I'm afraid I just don't have the answer," admitted Wynn. "We'll have to keep praying."

We both agonized over Henry. It was so important that he have love and grounding in order to be taught the truths of the Gospel and make his own decision to follow the Lord.

And yet, our Indian people were important, too. They needed someone to take the Gospel to them—and they needed it now.

I tried to leave it all with the Lord. "Cast your burden upon the Lord," the Scripture said, and I cast it—and then I pulled it back—and then I cast it again. I was miserable with my worrying, and then one day in my quiet prayer time I became honest, totally honest before God.

"Lord," I said, "I am sick of worrying about Henry. Now I know that I am not the only person that You can minister through. I give Henry over to You, Lord. If You ask us to leave him with someone else, then I am going to trust You that his needs will be met and that You will care for him—physically and spiritually.

"Help me to truly release him to You, knowing that You love and care for him. And help me not to take this burden of Henry's care back on my own shoulders again.

"Amen."

I finally found release. And strangely enough, instead of Henry seeming less important to me, as I had feared might happen, I loved him even more deeply. Still I did not fret about what would happen when the new orders came from the Police Head-quarters.

It was a Wednesday. Henry had come home from school, had his snack of cookies and milk, hurried through his chores with Kip fast on his heels, and then come to me with pleading in his eyes.

"Can I go over to the police office to play with the puppies and then walk home with Sergeant Wynn?" he asked me.

I wanted to correct him by saying, "May I," but I bit my tongue. Henry had so many things to learn that I must show patience.

He had developed a deep devotion for Wynn, and I knew it was good for him. I looked at the clock. I didn't want Henry getting in Wynn's way, but I knew he would be more than willing to play with the puppies until Wynn was ready to come home.

"I suppose you may," I told the eager Henry.

"Can I take Kip?" he asked next.

"Very well, take Kip. He needs a bit of a run. Make sure you keep him out of trouble. The sergeant won't take kindly to a dog fight in the street."

"I will," promised Henry, and he was off on a run, Kip bounding along ahead of him.

Henry had not been gone long when he was home again. He was all out of breath from his run, and his cheeks were flushed with excitement.

"Sergeant Wynn says to tell you that he will be another twenty minutes or so," he said, gasping for breath. "And he also said to tell you that we will have a guest for supper. A real live Indian. I saw him myself."

My excitement matched Henry's. Which one of our friends would be coming for supper? Was he from Beaver River or Smoke Lake? I could hardly wait to find out as I placed another plate on the table and checked to see if I would have enough meat and potatoes.

"I'm going back to walk home with them," said Henry, and he was off on a run again.

The time seemed to drag as I waited for Wynn and his guest to come for supper. I looked at the clock and then the road, over and over again.

When they finally did come, it was a stranger Wynn brought with him.

"Elizabeth," he said, "I want you to meet Pastor Walking Horse. He is from the village south of Smoke Lake. He has been out taking his training to become a minister to his own people."

My heart gave a flip.

"A pleasure to meet you, Mrs. Delaney," said the young man, and then he switched to the Indian tongue. "It gives me great joy to be a guest at your table."

Oh, it was so good to hear the flowing language again! I took his hand and shook it as the white man greets a friend, but my heart was crying out to him in the words of the Indian.

I welcome you to my fire, the words formed in my

mind. *My heart is glad for your presence. You make my joy increase as flowers after winter snows, and my soul sings like ripples of a brook with gladness.*

Henry was excited about sitting at the table with a real Indian. Wynn had told him much about the wisdom and the knowledge of the people in their own environment, and Henry had developed a healthy respect for them.

He listened now with Wynn and me as the young man explained how he had become acquainted in a personal way with the God of the Bible, and had cast aside all of the superstitious teachings of his forefathers in order to follow Him.

His desire now, he said, was to teach his people, and so he had gone out to take training and was ready to go back and challenge his people with the truth.

"My heart aches within me," he said sorrowfully, "because when I left my village to go to the white man's school, my chief said I would no longer be welcomed back, so I must go to another settlement to start my work."

"Ours," I said at once. "Ours. They are wonderful people, and they are ready, I'm sure. We have been praying and praying for someone to go to them. You are the answer to our prayers."

The man was almost as excited about this news as I was.

We talked on and on about the village and the people. Henry was finally scooted off to bed. He obeyed, but he went reluctantly. He hated to miss one word of the conversation.

We talked until long into the night, and by the time we were finished and had prayed together, Pastor Walking Horse was convinced that Smoke Lake was the place where the Lord was leading him, especially with LaMeche already a believer. He would try to be ready to leave as soon as the road was fit to travel.

Two days later Wynn came home from the office with a telegram in his hands. The Force had sent his new orders.

Much to the surprise of both of us, we were told we would be staying on at Athabasca Landing for the present time. The young Mountie at Smoke Lake would continue there at his post.

It came as a surprise to me, and yet it shouldn't have. I committed Henry to the Lord because I thought He would need me to care for the Indians. God had answered by preparing and sending a qualified young minister to the Indians and leaving Henry with me. I smiled. *One should never try to outguess the Lord*, I reminded myself.

"Well," I said to Wynn, "I guess God took care of it all in His own way. We wouldn't have needed to fret about it at all."

Wynn smiled and then kissed me.

"Do you mind, Elizabeth?" he asked.

I thought about that. I would miss our people. I

had been counting on going back—expecting to go back. But when I thought about it, I could answer honestly, "No, not really. It does seem best to stay for the present, doesn't it? The church needs us here. The Sunday school children need us. Then there is Henry. I expect great things from that boy someday, Wynn."

In a reflective moment I went on to answer Wynn's question.

"No, I don't mind. I guess I am quite content with God's direction in this."

I thought again about the village people.

"I will write a letter to Louis LaMeche and Silver Star," I said, "and send it with Pastor Walking Horse. I will tell Silver Star that she can have my garden. I will give them both our love and best wishes. Can I send her a few things—and Kinnea and Kinook, too?" I asked.

"I'm sure the pastor would be willing to take a few small gifts," said Wynn.

"You know," I pondered, "I might even write a short note to Chief Crow Calls Loud. Just a short note of introduction, telling him that he might be very interested in what Pastor Walking Horse has to say."

Wynn smiled again.

"So you will manage to run the village even from a distance, will you?" he teased.

I brushed aside his remark with a wave of my hand.

"Run it? No. But I certainly will continue to pray for those in it."

Then I turned to my cupboards.

"But right now I'd better get busy," I said, and there was love and joy in my voice. "I've a young boy due home from school in a few minutes, and he's always half-starved."

Children's Books by Janette Oke

Making Memories
Spunky's Camping Adventure
Spunky's Circus Adventure
Spunky's First Christmas

JANETTE OKE'S ANIMAL FRIENDS
(full-color for young readers)

Spunky's Diary
The Prodigal Cat
The Impatient Turtle
This Little Pig
New Kid in Town
Ducktails
Prairie Dog Town
Trouble in a Fur Coat
Maury Had a Little Lamb

CLASSIC CHILDREN'S STORIES
(for older readers)

Spunky's Diary	*A Cote of Many Colors*
The Prodigal Cat	*Prairie Dog Town*
The Impatient Turtle	*Trouble in a Fur Coat*
This Little Pig	*Maury Had a Little Lamb*
New Kid in Town	*Pordy's Prickly Problem*
Ducktails	*Who's New at the Zoo?*